BEBUQUIN

CARL EINSTEIN

BEBUQUIN

OR THE DILETTANTES
OF THE MIRACLE

TRANSLATED BY PATRICK HEALY

BILINGUAL EDITION

NOVEMBER EDITIONS
MMXVII

© 2017 November Editions/ Patrick Healy

This translation is based on the first edition of
Bebuquin oder die Dilettanten des Wunders published
in *Die Aktion* between July and October of in 1912.

Author portrait by Max Oppenheimer, 1912.

Cover design: Emma King

Typesetting: seagulls.net

ISBN 978-94-92027-12-2

November Editions – Amsterdam

For inquiries please contact us at hello@novembereditions.com

www.NovemberEditions.com

CONTENTS

INTRODUCTION

Carl Einstein once made a succinct and dramatic claim about the publication of *Bebuquin*: 'I was 20 and in literature.' This bald statement, which remains muted enough considering the extravagant precocity of the text, looks back at the salient fact of his literary debut in Berlin, where his engagement in the city's milieu of artists and writers remains one of the most fascinating and complex of the period, earning him the later sobriquet 'prophet of the avant-garde'.

Einstein was born in Neuwied on the 26th of April 1885, the son of Daniel and Sophie Einstein. In a 'little autobiography', reminiscent in its matter-of-fact tone of Hume's similarly terse report on his life, Einstein remarks on Karlsruhe, the capital of Baden to which the family moved in 1888, that it was very much 'on the wrong side of the Rhine'.[1] Even in the laconic, slightly melancholic intonation, one senses the profound pall of provincial boredom which made Einstein think of Karlsruhe as a city which seemed to be dying slowly. What really mattered for him in this time, he says, were the cowboy and Indian stories of Karl May, adding that the death of Winnetou was more important for him than that of Achilles, and still was in 1930, when he wrote the memoir. He left school before taking final exams, shortly after the death of his father in 1899, and tells of spending Sunday evening getting drunk, and reading detective stories, Wedekind and Rimbaud.

It was a time of quirky meetings, and an extravagant cast of characters make a fleeting appearance in his short text: a living poet introduced by a barmaid, a professor of physics who didn't believe in gravity and a Messiah who hailed from Bordeaux, probably of Turkish origin, and was a heavy drinker with an impressive knowledge of harbour cities. Abruptly this is followed by the remark: 'Then I went to Berlin.' He was still a teenager.

In Berlin Einstein at first lived as a lodger with Frau Zilinsky in the Borsigstrasse, between the students and the *Kokotten*. After six months he moved to Potsdamer Platz, and then rapidly and dryly notes how he met Ludwig Rubiner in the university, and discussed adventure novels in the evening. Einstein had brought 34 volumes of the popular crime fiction series *Fantômas* from Paris, his favourites being *Le Pendu de Londres*, and *Le Fiacre de nuit*.

> Then I wrote *Bebuquin*; Blei printed it in the *Opale*, and so one was twenty and in literature.

Remarkably it is this fact on which he ends the autobiography, which indicates perhaps the sense of fate he attached to this publication.

At university he also formed the beginning of a life-long friendship with Gottfried Benn, whose publishers were among the first to create an Einstein edition, and revival, after the Second World War. Benn is quoted as saying in 1951:

> I often think of Einstein and read his books. He had it,
> he really was at the top. Those were the genius years of
> Germany, 1912-33, maybe the last Germany had.

The Berlin of 1904, where Einstein enrolled for university courses in philosophy, art history, and history, included attendance at the lectures of Georg Simmel, the chief conduit for Bergsonism in Germany. The famous paper on 'The Metropolis and Mental Life' which Simmel delivered around that time registers in precise detail the sense of the enormous increase in the intensification of the nervous life of city inhabitants, with people being forced through the impersonality of the city, the place of punctuality and rational impersonal economic exchange, to behave in a blasé way in order to deal with the new experiences of shock and distraction, which the very functioning of the metropolis creates, whilst in tandem increasing their capacity for discrimination. The city is the place of endless 'shocks' and self-protection; the latter often presented itself as paralysis, whilst the former would result in surrealism.

Simmel clearly has Berlin in mind, the city that for such a long time had been between a ruin and a building site. In his review of Karl Scheffler's book *Berlin: ein Stadtschicksal* (1910), the art historian Max Raphael fastened on the phrase that the Berliner had been 'doomed always to becoming and never to be'. Raphael then invokes a more complex metaphor: 'he is the modern Ahasverus, perpetually wandering and restless.'[2]

The theme of 'the young man from the provinces' as a major subject of 19th-century fiction is well exemplified in the ferocious energy and achievements of Einstein. From his interest and lifestyle one can see the generational revolt 'against the fathers' that has been taken as such a mark of this period. Apart from attending lectures, the erratic and brilliant Einstein was also a regular in the café society of the Café des Westens, where he went every afternoon at 4 p.m. and was usually in the company of, among others, George Grosz, the art dealer Alfred Flechtheim, the sculptor de Fiori and the artist Rudolf Belling; and not far from their habitual seating place was the table of the generation of older painters and artists such as Max Liebermann, Max Slevogt, Emil Orlik and Heinrich Zille. This localises the second level of generational conflict, a conflict between the younger and older artists, with the younger generation being in open revolt. A wonderful evocation of this café life can be found in the almost contemporary publication of Else Lasker-Schüler's *roman à clef* titled *Mein Herz.*[3]

Einstein also had direct connections with the group involved in the periodical *Die Aktion*, who described themselves as left of the communists. *Bebuquin,* the text that established Einstein's reputation, had started its life as *Herr Giorgio Bebuquin* in Franz Blei's publication *Die Opale*, in 1907,[4] but the full text would eventually be published in serial form in *Die Aktion* during the second half of 1912, under the title *Bebuquin oder die Dilettanten des Wunders.*[5] It is on this version of the text that the current translation is based. The serialisation is preceded by a dedication to André Gide, which also gives dates for the composition of the work: 'Für André Gide. Geschrieben 1906/9' (For André Gide. Written 1906/9). At the end of 1912, after the appearance of the last instalment in *Die Aktion*, the text was moreover issued in book form by the journal's publishing imprint (Die Aktion Verlag), again as *Bebuquin oder die Dilettanten des Wunders*, while a second edition simply called *Bebuquin* would follow in 1917.

When *Bebuquin* was being published in *Die Aktion*, the chief editor was Franz Pfemfert, who was to become Einstein's brother-in-law in 1913. The periodical had been responsible for publishing Franz Mehring, Rosa Luxembourg and Bakunin, and these would remain Einstein's life-long political loyalties, as evidenced by the fact that he would later volunteer as a soldier in the Spanish Civil War, fighting on the side of the anarchist Durutti column. The full list of contributors to *Die Aktion* reads as a roll call of the most advanced intellectual tendencies of the period that would come to be known as the epoch of Expressionism. It included Paul Adler, Kurt Hiller, Alfred Wolfenstein, Franz Jung, Rudolph Leonard, Gottfried Benn, Ferdinand Hardekopf and Max Raphael.

It was Max Raphael who, in 1911, wrote the very first article in German using the term 'Der Expressionismus'.[6] In the article Raphael defends the young generation of painters against the attacks of Lovis Corinth, who had described them as imitators of Cézanne, Van Gogh and Gauguin. Raphael names the new tendency from the work of Pechstein, Purmann, Levy, Kirchner, Heckel and Schmidt-Rottluff, among the Germans, and Picasso, Matisse and van Dongen among the foreigners. According to Raphael, for these artists the new ideal is the picture, creating a structure independent in itself, free from alien connections. It is the picture, and not nature, which dictates the laws of creation: 'The difference between every Expressionism and every Naturalism lies in the will to create.' For the modern artist the absolute is no longer to be sought behind the relative, but rather the relative has to be transformed into clarity and necessity. Nothing objective can constitute the creative point of view, for the artist knows with the surety of subjective experience that there is no objective certainty: 'He can be led by his personal sensation alone.'

The peculiarity which Raphael notes in this position is that the sensation always emerges anew from the contact with the object, that is, not in a stylisation, but in a will to style. The world of forms does not exist a priori, nor forces objects into shapes; rather it comes into being each time out of the tension between subject and object; it is not a schema but active formation. What occurs is a simultaneity of reception, re-working and representation which leads to greater clarity and simplicity, more expression, more of what is personal. The Expressionists mistrust the impression, and seek to raise it to an unambiguous, clear, simple and necessary concept. This involves abstraction, and against Impressionism with its spreading, open continuity, they aim at the 'self-containment of the picture'. It is, as Raphael says, to be concluded that the imitation of nature is actually not the constituent mark of visual art. It is precisely this anti-mimesis which is also crucial for Einstein's strategy in his poetics.

For German Expressionist literature one could almost name the young Berlin university friends Einstein and Benn as the principle source. The short chapters and the remarkable compression of *Bebuquin* make expression itself the chief feature of the work, since summarising the text is fated to be impossible and the question of meaning must remain undecided. There is a sense in which the book destroys the tradition of realist fictions, and yet it designates itself as a 'novel', although it could equally be described as a meta-fiction. It is a *Blitzbuch* and its appearance gained Einstein immediate recognition, and ultimately a place among the leading authors of German literature from the first half of the twentieth century. Indeed, along with Gottfried Benn and Franz Jung, Einstein would be identified as exemplary for Expressionist writing in Albert Soergel's 1925 anthology *Im Banne des Expressionismus*, a view that would be repeated in Karl Otten's influential 1957 anthology *Ahnung und Aufbruch: Expressionistische Prosa*.[7]

This does not square however with the earliest reception of *Bebuquin*, as exemplified in Kurt Hiller's review in *Pan*, a rival journal to *Die Aktion*, which appeared in 1912.[8] Hiller commented on the 'decadent' figure of Bebuquin, since Franz Blei, who had supported the early version of the text in his journal *Die Opale*, had a specialist interest in French erotic literature and in his independent publication *Rokoko* included essays on Restif de la Bretonne and Sade. Moreover, Blei's other magazine *Hyperion* carried Beardsley erotica, was produced on Japanese paper and issued as a deluxe publication, and at the time of the appearance of Einstein's text, Blei had just published a monograph on Félicien Rops, the most modish evocation of symbolism in painting. It is evident that the 'decadent' atmosphere of *Bebuquin* makes for easy comparison with Hofmannsthal's 'Letter of Lord Chandos', the unproductive narcissus, and indeed the aristocrat aesthete Des Esseintes of Huysman's *A Rebours*, who is finally absorbed by his own *akrasia*.

In 1928 Einstein met his future second wife Lyda Guévrékian and settled in Paris. In the French capital he co-founded the art magazine *Documents* with Georges Bataille, and collaborated with Eugene Jolas on the journal *transition*, which would feature an English-language translation of the sixth chapter of *Bebuquin* in 1929.[9] In his modest and immensely readable memoirs *Man from Babel*, Jolas leaves a captivating pen-picture of Einstein.[10] Einstein had often encouraged him to visit Berlin, to collect 'the last echoes of the Expressionist era' before they became buried in 'nationalistic realism'. He had informed Jolas of the new and dangerous jingoism emerging in Germany, remarking that the Prussian spirit was not dead, and adding: 'Expressionism was the last form of the human equation in Germany.' In the work of another younger generation Einstein saw nothing but the drift towards Teutonic megalomania, the sterile echo of the creative mind, epigones who might become dangerous to European peace. Noting the dangerous mixture of sentimentalism and power-lust in the German, Einstein, as reported in Jolas, was still convinced that there were a few humanists left who would prevent the Teuton-beserk spirit from gaining the upper hand, suggesting that Thomas Mann, whom he did not like, might have enough influence to be the brake on young writers evolving towards military nationalism.

For some time Jolas, Hans Arp and Einstein met in Einstein's book-cluttered apartment near the Boulevard de Grenelle, talking about poetry in the German language and indulging in 'grandiose plans for a collection of poetry plaquettes to be issued'. In true combative mode and with his fine anarchic intelligence, Einstein wanted to launch a cry of revolt against what he called the spirit of Fichte among the German poets. 'Let's hurl something in their faces,' he said. 'The two or three poets left there will thank us.'

However, most of Einstein's indignation focused on Goethe, his true *bête noire* among the German writers, against whom he would launch a furious broadside. Vitriolic remarks included describing Goethe as 'the greatest bore on the European continent, that ruined antiquarian of letters', and, 'the little burgher who worked to preserve his fame after his death.' Jolas took Einstein at his word, and asked him to prepare an article for the hundredth anniversary of Goethe's death, which he went at, according to Jolas 'hammer and tongs'.[11] It is in this contribution on Goethe that one finds Einstein's sustained literary position. Analysing the text also helps to understand the strange eruption of the work of *Bebuquin*, as clearly exemplifying Einstein's deepest creative convictions.

Briefly one can say that the plot of *Bebuquin*, even in the scenario-like chapter treatment, is that Giorgio Bebuquin, the snobbish young poet, although akrasic wants to create something specific, something out of himself without any influences. He meets the director of the Museum of Cheap Thrills, during the annual fair, and Böhm, the Thinker with the silver engraved skull, who reappears as a ghost after his sudden death. Bebuquin tries to achieve his goal, one drink at a time, while he meets up with the actress Fredegonde Perlenblick, the painter Heinrich Lippenknabe, and the 'Platonist' Ehmke Laurenz. Bebuquin 'gets' religion and goes to a cloister where he self-induces a form of destruction through a created sickness that leads to madness, which also spreads to a whole group of people to whom he is a mirror reflection, 'for still the glimmering terror of the mirror hung over the city.' All of this is entwined through a rapid hallucination, without characters in any traditional sense, but more as expressive modes of a fragmenting artefactual figure.

One needs to look at the later writing of Einstein to grasp what happened in this hypothetical action, erupting event, called *Bebuquin*. Arguably, Einstein creates a literary text that achieves the *focus imaginarius*, where everything in the text is a becoming, and in which the process of dissolution and metamorphosis breaks with the novelistic tradition of realist and narrative-bound works. It is possible to argue that there is an analogy with Cubist technique in the work, which implies the dissolution and regrouping of the space/time sense for the personality, in other words the creation of a phenomenal time and space would devastate a linear-time continuum and static notions of space.

The idea of qualitative time implied for Einstein a multitude of multiple qualitative discontinuums; past, present and future dissolve into a complex time experience which is the decisive metaphoric character of the work. As in Cubism, there is a spatial and temporal simultaneity of diverging views and a simultaneous complex of transitory figuration and transformation. This culminates in the destruction of discrete determined objects; Einstein abandons the notion of a substantial 'I', and the synthetic centre of all the transformations and figurations of *Bebuquin* is the made-up, artefactual performance of the work itself. The tension between the artifical and the phantastic, even phantasmic, in the thematic of the work is played out around the hypothetical action of a funeral wake, concluding, if it concludes, in the brief report on the laying out of the corpse of the chief protagonist.

Bebuquin deploys a fictive 'I'. There is no stable self to distribute into second-order fictions, for the fictive subject is one in the process of unfolding, within the folds of the text itself, and can break out and implore within the text: 'O Lord, grant me a miracle; we have been seeking it since chapter one.' This request for a miracle is our own situation, the desire for the 'event', and our asking: 'will it happen?'

But it is not just reversals and reflective distortions that are at play. That would not deroute the substantive and controlling discourse under attack; if anything it would merely serve to strengthen it. The strategy of the writer is not that he simply smashes the isomorphisms that are meant to be constitutive of meaning everywhere in the world. Rather, he is involved in a process that depends on a complex interplay between simulacrum, deception and the permanent un-reality of the image, its ceaseless struggle to refer, where it is real only on the basis of its non-reality. It is this disjunction that implies the philosophical grotesque throughout. The magic dramaturgy of meaning morphs into a melodic madness. Joyce too had a brilliant metaphor for the condition of loss and absurdity – the cracked mirror.

The swingeing polemic against Goethe in *transition* turns on a central point: Goethe has avoided contact with the dangerously immediate present. He was a ridiculous optimist, exhibiting an offensive serenity, inane moderation, and displaying all the insouciant values of a rococo aristocrat. Goethe refuses to confront death and decay, preferring to wallow in a lazy and conflict-free notion of unity, espouse an idiotic hedonism. He feared the real; insanity and death were for him offensive odours. Likewise Goethe degenerated eroticism into respectability and his ideal of cheerful Hellenism never suspected for a moment the hallucinative root of early antiquity, what Einstein calls the 'sacred dementia'. Faust, after all, ends up as a property developer.

What Goethe never sensed, was the problematic and murderous nature of art, preferring, like Shaw, to go whore-mongering among a few false optimistic ideas. Einstein's fundamental position is then shown when he accuses Goethe of overlooking the hypothetical element of all creation, the element which alone allows cognition to gain independence and power. Here Einstein's argument is that the artist insists on the hallucinative process of his own subjectivity. It was in this sense for him that freedom could be gained, and that the work was a hypothetical action.

The subjective could be quickened into form through the process of hallucinative seeing, where the elements of vertiginous subjectivity, free fantasy, the grotesque of a logic of sensation, would free the writer or artist from the tyranny of the mimetic. Einstein registered viscerally the overbearing demands that the stabilising of the world into subject and object created, and out of writing wanted to create a meta-object, away from the static and unrelieved character of the ontological which resulted in a double making both subject and object a thing. The full engagement of lived experience was ultimately pre-theoretical, and involved a necessary destruction of previous epistemological commitments.

The grotesque in the psychological realm opened the real, the domain of succession and simultaneity. It could even generate figures, through the transpersonal that resulted from the creation of the meta-object, a prose work; thus, the dilettante, the narcissus, the snob in their sterility generate the search for the creative in the text itself. The grotesque contains, as Ruskin once observed, the ludicrous and the fearful. *Bebuquin* is grotesque even in the name, invented, childish, absurd.

Indeed one can see that what Goethe cannot accomplish could be read as Einstein's achievement. There is a hypothetical element in all creation, and Goethe never dares the mad leap, as Einstein calls it, the leap into the symbol, which at least characterises the conflict between man and being. Goethe remains possessed of the regnant delusion of the Enlightenment, that all existence develops according to law.

Because cognition, of which hypothesis is the marked characteristic, develops a-logically and unconsciously, it takes on a fatal appearance, and thus seems necessary to us. It is the fatal automatism of the unconscious which casts its shadow over the event, the irruption of being as presence, its understanding as event, what emerges in a living, non-theoretical way, and indeed cognition is feared because its origins remain unknown to us, and all faith in logic is rooted in the fear of our own automatism.

Every continuity is woven out of a fear of death, and against the harmonic Hellenism of Goethe, Einstein invokes a new quantum where the unity of the real is displaced by the dialectical pluralism of reality. For Einstein the words of power were the primitive, metamorphosis, the ecstatic. In his absurd optimism Goethe failed to understand that every act is ecstatic and can only come about through the destruction of the 'I'.

Cognition is a form of destruction. In the substraction of perception, which is always less and more than what it feels, the contraction of energy is the form itself, a diminution of living contacts, an elimination of conventional reality, and paradoxically the creation of a new *mythos*. It cannot be enough, as at the end of Faust, to conjure a fraudulent *jouissance*, an artificial hallucination, instead of taking the courage of a position to creative dying. Instead, Goethe launches rockets of dead allegories, remaining a stranger forever to the fatal necessity of Hölderlin. The only myth Goethe created was of his own well-organised fame.

For Einstein all philosophical idealism was a kind of madness, a phobia towards the concrete, and aesthetic theory a kind of defence against the 'provisorium' of the artwork. The grotesque as the booth of distorting mirrors was the consequence of the limit of the human experience.

The dazzling literary debut that was *Bebuquin* would remain the only novel Einstein published. His subsequent publications, including *Negerplastik* in 1915 and the first overview of twentieth-century art, *Die Kunst des 20. Jahrhunderts* in 1926,[12] would establish him as a pivotal figure in the articulation of European Modernism and arguably the most influential art critic of the early-twentieth century. The present translation of *Bebuquin* – the first integral English-language edition to appear to date – allows the contemporary reader to experience first-hand the radical innovative energy of the young Einstein, a force which remains undiminished more than a century after the book's original appearance.

NOTES

1. All these details can be found in *Carl Einstein. Prophet der Avantgarde*, ed. Klaus Siebenhaar (Berlin: Fannei & Walz Verlag, 1991); see especially the 'Kleine Autobiographie' at pp.12-15. Also see Conor Joyce, *Carl Einstein in Documents and his Collaboration with George Bataille* (Xlibris, 2003).

2. The text appeared under the pseudonym M.R. Schönlank as 'Die Weltstadt Berlin', in *Nord und Sud*, XXXV, vol.135, H.6 (2nd September issue, 1910), pp.506-509. For my translation into English see Max Raphael, *The Invention of Expressionism: Critical Writings 1910-1913*, ed. and trans. Patrick Healy (November Editions, 2016), pp. 66-71.

3. Else Lasker-Schüler's *Mein Herz* was first serialised as *Briefe nach Norwegen* in *Der Sturm*, 1911-12, and then appeared in book form (Munich: Heinrich F.S. Bachmair, 1912). It was translated into English by Sheldon Gilman and Robert Levine as *My Heart: A Novel of Love* (November Editions, 2016).

4. *Die Opale*, 2, (1907), pp.169-175.

5. For a list of Einstein's publications, see the bibliography in *Text+Kritik*, 95, pp.90-94.

6. The text appeared under the pseudonym M.R. Schönlank, 'Der Expressionismus', in *Nord und Sud*, XXXV, vol. 138, H.437 (1st September issue, 1911), pp.360-365. For my translation into English see Max Raphael, *The Invention of Expressionism: Critical Writings 1910-1913*, *op. cit.*, pp.113-121.

7. *Dichtung und Dichter der Zeit. Neue Folge – Im Banne des Expressionismus*, ed. Albert Soergel (Leipzig: Voigtländers Verlag, 1925); *Ahnung und Aufbruch: Expressionistische Prosa*, ed. Karl Otten (Darmstadt: Luchterhand Verlag, 1957).

8. A collection of contemporary reviews and comments on *Bebuquin* can be found in *Carl Einstein, Materialien*, Band 1, *Zwischen* Bebuquin *und* Negerplastik, ed. Rolf-Peter Baacke (Berlin: Silver & Goldstein, 1990), pp.49-79.

9. The translation was prepared by Jolas and published in *transition*, 16-17 (1929).

10. Eugene Jolas, *Man from Babel*, ed. Andreas Kramer and Rainer Rumold (New Haven: Yale University Press, 1998). For bibliographical indications and details of Jolas, see Dougald McMillan, *Transition 1927-38: The History of a Literary Era* (London: Calder and Boyars, 1975).

11. I have drawn directly from *Man from Babel, op. cit.*

12. Carl Einstein, *Negerplastik* (Leipzig: Weissen Bücher Verlag, 1915); available in English as *Negro Sculpture*, trans. Patrick Healy (November Editions, 2016); *Die Kunst des 20. Jahrhunderts* (Berlin: Propyläen Verlag, 1926).

CHRONOLOGY

1885   Carl Einstein is born (as *Karl* Einstein) in the German town of Neuwied, near Karlsruhe in the province of Baden, on 26 April. He is the second child of author, administrator and cantor Daniel Einstein and Sophie Einstein (née Lichtenstein). His sister Hedwig, who is one year older, will become a concert pianist.

1888   The family moves to nearby Karlsruhe, living in relatively prosperous conditions.

1894   Einstein attends the Karlsruhe Bismarck-Gymnasium.

1899   Death of Einstein's father after prolonged nervous illness. Reduced circumstances for the family.

1903   Leaves school abruptly without his diploma. Works in a local bank and after a few months departs for Berlin.

1904   Enrols in courses at Berlin's Friedrich-Wilhelms University, among which art-history, philosophy, history and philology. Attends philosophy lectures on Kant and Schopenhauer given by Georg Simmel and Alois Riehl. Riehl had just published his introduction to contemporary philosophy, *Zur Einführung in die*

Philosophie der Gegenwart, which will become a continuous target, as well as a source, throughout *Bebuquin*. At this time Simmel also delivers his famous lecture on 'The Metropolis and Mental Life'. Among Einstein's other teachers are Ulrich von Wilamowitz-Moellendorff, an early opponent of Nietzsche and Germany's pre-eminent classicist, and Heinrich Wölfflin, whose courses on art historical principles he attends.

1907 Publication of *Herr Giorgio Bebuquin* in Franz Blei's journal *Die Opale*. Trip to Paris, where he discovers and meets with Picasso, Braque and Gris. The art dealer Kahnweiler has been at the same Gymnasium as Einstein and welcomes him to the Paris scene.

1908 Leaves university after five semesters. Publishes his *Verwandlungen*, based on four legends, in the journal *Hyperion*.

1910 Franz Blei introduces Einstein to Kurt Hiller and Franz Pfemfert. His first writing on art appears in the journal *Demokraten*, which Pfemfert left over censorship disputes to found the new weekly *Die Aktion*.

1912 Between July and October *Bebuquin oder die Dilettanten des Wunders* is serialised in *Die Aktion*. Later in the year it is published in book form by Die Aktion Verlag.

1913 Marriage to the Russian translator Maria Ramm, whose sister Alexandra is married to Franz Pfemfert. Gives reading performances at author evening events of *Die Aktion*, including lectures on contemporary painting. Writes to the director of the Völkerkunde Museum in Berlin to propose a special issue of the review *Der Merker* on Negro sculpture and Mexican art. In November collaborates on an exhibition at the Neue Gallerie showing works of Picasso, Derain and Matisse, including a room devoted to African sculpture.

1914   Volunteers for military service at the outbreak of World War I. Sustains serious head injury in November, and recuperates over the following months until May, assembling *Negerplastik* for publication during his convalescence.

1915   The Weissen Bücher Verlag in Leipzig publishes *Negerplastik*.

1916   Transfers to Belgium to the Colonial Department of the Gouvernement Général de Bruxelles. Research at the Museée du Congo at Tervuren. His collection of essays, including one on Beckford's *Vathek*, is published under the title *Anmerkungen* by the Die Aktion Verlag.

1917   The second edition of *Bebuquin* is published by Die Aktion Verlag. Einstein is sent back to the Front, where he sustains further injuries and trauma. Denounced for political reasons and demobbed.

1918   Publication of *Der unentwegte Platoniker. Drei Erzählungen* by Kurt Wolff Verlag in Leipzig. Einstein participates in the 'November Revolution' in Brussels. Red flag flown on 10 November. Returns to Berlin and participates in the Revolutionary Soldiers Council.

1919   Arrested on the day when Rosa Luxemburg and Karl Liebknecht are murdered. He gives the funeral oration for Rosa Luxemburg. Contributes to the satirical publication *Die Pleite*, and works with George Grosz on the journal *Der blutige Ernst*, issues 3-6. The publication will be shut down for political reasons.

1921   Publication of *Afrikanische Plastik* by Wasmuth Verlag in Berlin, a more scholarly and annotated work than *Negerplastik*. Publication of *Die schlimme Botschaft* by Rowohlt Verlag in Berlin, a play dealing with the crucifixion of Jesus set partly in Germany.

1922   *Die schlimme Botschaft* is tried under blasphemy laws. Einstein and his publisher are found guilty and fined 15,000 Marks. Booklet publication on *Der frühere japanische Holzschnitt* by Wasmuth Verlag in Berlin. Recognised as a major figure in art criticism and commissioned to write an overview of twentieth-century art by Propyläen Verlag.

1923   Booklet publication on the painter Moishe Kisling, a close friend of Einstein, in the series *Junge Kunst* issued by Klinkhardt & Biermann in Leipzig.

1925   Publication of *Afrikanische Märchen und Legenden* by Rowohlt Verlag in Berlin.

1926   The first overview book on twentieth-century art, *Die Kunst des 20. Jahrhunderts*, appears with Propyläen Verlag. It will go to a third edition in 1931.

1927   Booklet publication on painter and designer Léon Bakst by Ernst Wasmuth Verlag in Berlin.

1928   Leaves Germany and moves to Paris.

1929   Founds the journal *Documents* with Georges Bataille and publisher of renown Georges Wildenstein. Meets ethnologist and writer Michel Leiris. Chapter six of *Bebuquin* published in *transition* in an English-language translation by Eugene Jolas.

1930 Booklet publication on Giorgio de Chirico by the Flechtheim gallery in Berlin. Publication of the poem *Entwurf einer Landschaft*, with illustrations by Gaston-Louis Roux, by Editions Galerie Simon in Paris.

1932 Second marriage, to Lyda Guévrékian. Georges Braque serves as a witness.

1934 Publication of the monograph *Georges Braque* by Editions des chroniques du jour in Paris. Works with Jean Renoir on the script for the film *Toni* (released 1935).

1936 Goes to Barcelona to fight on behalf of the anarcho-syndicalists. In combat under Durruti. Gives funeral oration for Durruti on November 22.

1939 Flees Spain for Paris.

1940 Interred in Bordeaux, released in June. Collapse of the Third Republic. Drowns himself by jumping in the river in the town of Lestelle-Bétharram on 5 July.

BEBUQUIN

For André Gide
Written 1906/9

CHAPTER ONE

Splinters of a glass yellow lamp clattered from the voice of the slattern: 'Do you want to see your mother's ghost?' The unsteady light dripped onto the filigree bald head of a young man who shifted anxiously, to avoid all reflections concerning the makeup of his person. He turned away from the booth of distorting mirrors which give rise to more observations than the speeches of fifteen professors. He turned away from the Circus of Suspended Gravity and, laughing, realised that he thereby would let slip the solution to his life. He also avoided the Theatre of Dumb Ecstasy with his proudly bent head: for all ecstasy is obscene, ecstasy ridicules our abilities; and he went trembling into the Museum of Cheap Thrills where an excessive large lady sat naked at the cash desk. She was so big she couldn't sit on a chair, only on her dejected enormous posterior. She wore a wide-brimmed hat with yellow feathers, and emerald colour stockings whose garters went all the way up to her armpits, and decorated her body with fairly lifeless arabesques. From her seal hands red rubies stared perpendicularly. 'Good evening, Herr Bebuquin,' she said. Bebuquin entered the dingily lit room where a big fat doll with rouge and painted eyebrows was standing, which from the very beginning had been trying to blow a kiss. As he was delighted by the unartistic he sat on a stool just a little stretch away from the doll. The young man didn't know what it was about the unartistic which was so compelling for him. He found a quite friendly numbness to which he was indifferent. What always got him was the remarkable fact that this conventional calm smile could render him unconscious. Because he hadn't died off in sufficient degree to be taken as a charming person, he was capable of being angered by the silence of lifeless things. He screamed at the doll, cursed her, and once again threw her from her chair and out the door where the fat lady picked her up with care. He went into the empty parlour: 'I don't want to be a copy, no influence, I want myself, I want something unique from my own soul, something individual, even if it is only holes in the private air. I can't start anything with things, one thing involves all other things. It stays in flux and the infinity of a point is a horror.'

The fat lady, Fräulein Euphemia, came and beseeched him to continue as a fatter gentleman yelled:

'Young fellow why don't you busy yourself with the exact sciences?'

Painfully it dawned on him that he who had wanted to see a performance was a show for someone else. He screamed out:

'I am a mirror, a motionless puddle glittering with reflected gaslight. But has a mirror ever mirrored itself?'

The corpulent one looked with sympathy. He had a small head, the silver skull of which was decorated with wonderfully engraved ornaments in which luminous plates of precious stones were inlaid. Giorgio wanted to flee but Nebukadnezar Böhm screamed at him angrily:

'What are you jumping around in my atmosphere for, you beast?'

'Excuse me, sir, but your atmosphere is the product of factors which have no relation to you.'

'Even so,' Nebukadnezar replied gently, 'it is a question of power, a matter of naming and self-hypnosis.'

Bebuquin straightened himself.

'You are surely from Saxony and have read Nietzsche, who went mad because he wasn't trusted with a police job and by force of circumstance had to write psychologically nuanced books.'

Fräulein Euphemia begged the men to treat her spirit in a more rational fashion, and she would be happy to go to a nightclub. They both nodded and pounded down the stairs.

Euphemia collected her night-wrap, and Nebukadnezar grabbed a megaphone and bellowed into the vast receding Milky Way:

'I'm looking for a miracle.' Euphemia's lapdog tumbled out of the megaphone and Euphemia came back again with a pleasant smile.

'Darling,' intoned Nebukadnezar, 'the erotic is the ecstasy of dilettantes, but I will sponsor you in my next *feuilleton*. Women are always exhausting; they continually offer the same thing, and we never wish to believe that two completely different bodies possess the same centre.'

'Adieu, I will not prevent you from proving your observations through action.'

Euphemia requested the fat one to order something to eat and drink from the Hotel and turned round to care for her dog about whose accident she had heard. The fat one grabbed a tree and clutched his throat. Then out he went to look after the dog. –

Nebukadnezar bent his head over the massive breast of Euphemia. A mirror was hanging over him. He saw how her bosom divided and exploded in multiple strange forms in the finely polished precious stones of his head, in forms which no reality had previously shown him. The chased silver broke up and refined the sparkle of the shapes. Nebukadnezar stared at the mirror with avaricious delight at his ability to dissect reality, at his soul being silver and jewels, his eyes the mirror. 'Bebuquin!' he screamed as he broke down, for he still wished to bear the soul of things. Two arms hauled him up and pressed him on two large teats and long strands of hair fell onto his silver skull, and every hair was a thousand forms. He remembered the woman and noticed uneasily that he couldn't reach her through the glitter of the jewels and his body almost burst in the struggle of two realities. Then he was seized by wild joy because his silver brain lent him almost immortality in that it raised all appearance to a higher power, and he could close down his thinking thanks to the precise cut of the stones and the completely logical engraving. With the forms of the engravings he could create a new logic whose visible symbol was the scratches of the capsule. It increased his power and he believed in an other, always new world, with ever new pleasures. He no longer realised his body in the almost forgotten sense of touch which meandered in pain and with which the visible world was not in agreement.

'Don't abuse me, please,' the thin voice of Bebuquin sounded in the mirror. 'Don't let yourself get so excited by objects, it is only a combination, not something new. Don't rave with misplaced means. Where are you then? We can't jump out of our skins. The whole matter unfolds itself with a strict causality. Yes, if logic would release us, at what point would its insertion be; that is what neither of us know. That is where the best is. You almost become original because you almost become insane. Let us sing the song of common loneliness. Your search for originality comes from your shameless emptiness, mine also. I will excuse myself without further ado, then you can mirror yourself in yourself. You see, that is the rub. But things do not bring us any further.'

The lace curtains were pulled across.

CHAPTER TWO

Bebuquin tossed in the pillows and suffered.

He tried to discover, firstly, what suffering might be, and how suffering might bring him a reason, a purpose. But he found none, for when he dismembered his pain he found fundamentals, or, more precisely, metamorphoses, which were completely other than pain. He recognised suffering as a stimulus to joy, as an agreeable releasing, and then told himself that there was nowhere that suffering could be found, and the entire bestowing of names was a laughable and naïve confusion; for the logical has nothing to do with the spiritual: that is false accounting. That was as bad as a painter who represented virtue as a blonde slut.

'The mistake of the logical is that it can never count as symbolic. One must understand, you fools, that logic can only be a style, without ever being based on any kind of reality. We must compose logically, from logical figures, like ornament designers. We must realise that the phantastic is logic.'

Boredom overwhelmed him when he thought of objects which wanted to absorb him, how he had annihilated objects with his symbolic system, and how everything only existed in the extermination. Here he saw a justification for every aesthetic, but also could see no teleology, and that the individual must be denied. He longed for insanity, but unrestrained remaining humanity was terrified. It seemed to him his only salvation lay in a kind of decent *ennui,* but not to use it like the jolly Schopenhauer as a sneak justification for the system. It was clear to him that in *ennui* there was a latent principle of style of the first order. It gave him enormous pleasure to kick around with infinity when browsing in maths books as children play with balls and hoops. He believed that here there was no passing over into the thing, he noted that he was in himself.

He saw clearly that it was a big mistake to call oneself a poet, for in art one always remains in the intoxication of symbols. It didn't satisfy him at all that the technique of poetry might be symbolic and that the subject could contain a completely other sense, and he still found that linguistic representation was an impure act when measured against music. He detested the efforts of academics to lead the conception of music back to the idea of real physiological antecedents. He was pleased by the fact that they were only interpreting their own alimentary system, avoiding all art with great sureness. It thrilled him to discover the confirmation of an old truth that the part in respect of the whole has absolutely nothing to say, that the unconscious precondition for the logical was the synthetic, and that one missed the main point just as the psychologist had.

Sadly he called out: 'What rotten novelistic material I am: I will never do anything for I revolve around in myself; I would like to say something clever about action, if only I knew what it was. I am certain I have never dealt with or experienced it.'

'Never enjoyed anything either, you fool,' hissed Nebukadnezar in the parlour and closed again the lid of the chamber-pot. Luminous little clouds glowed and a muslin curtain covered with delicate flowers was drawn apart.

'Sir, you are blathering about a pure detachment from yourself. I notice you are seeking God. Yes, I will admit that it is difficult to comprehend that everything relative will become absolute through pleasure and similar passive inebriations. You haven't yet managed to forget the way to things, but, you suckling calf with the philosopher's brow, the results are the same,' he screamed with his raised index finger. 'I have never taken any interest in what I am enjoying, but that I am enjoying has always been of the greatest importance to me.'

'Sir, you are seeking purposes with your stomach. Please leave. Anyway your transcendental pleasure machine was dangerous. I was present at your holy leave-taking.'

'You still don't see that the nerve-ends were torn apart. The engraved brain was much more durable. It is outrageous that your fake seriousness always encourages me to make bad jokes. Now you have your own unique reflection.'

He sat down beside Bebuquin in the bed.

'Bebuquin,' he said gently, 'you are still a human being. Vary yourself a little, you monotonous clump. Allow me to relate to you the story of the curtains from the Garden of Signs. Narcissus, the unproductive one.'

Giorgio pulled the blankets off his ears, put a cake in his mouth and Böhm began:

CHAPTER THREE
THE STORY OF THE CURTAINS

I stood before a large piece of sackcloth and shouted: 'You are but knots.'

'Must you always swear?'

'Don't interrupt me. I need to verify myself. I soon noticed that the sackcloth was none other than myself. That was the first self-awareness. But I pushed on further. A great rumbling began. A storm tore me apart. I howled from pain. I observed that the largest part of the sackcloth had gone 'phut'. Then I became completely blinded by myself. Think of this: I was a steel mountain standing on its tip. Tender blooms of the soul covered the abysses which couldn't have been filled with baby-pink sofa cushions. I grasped the complete nonsense and realised that a gram of sand was worth far more than an endless world. It dawned on me that the infinitesimal, the miracle of quality, cannot be dissolved by history, or anything else for that matter. Anyway, what I took from this was that it derives from the most effortless possible movement. I confess that in this case logic doesn't go far enough because each axiom contradicts the other. Think of this then: the proposition of causal thinking leads precisely to the non-causal, yet nevertheless, with green humility, I go for the main thing. I said to myself, Böhm, abandon yourself. Everything that is personal is unproductive. Be a curtain and tear yourself apart. Nag at yourself so long that you are something else. Be the curtain and the performance at the same time. When you have a desire, go in the opposite direction; otherwise you will get stuck in the mud. I have always said that reversal is equally correct. But don't go around any more on two legs. Why not heroically amputate one of them under the bed-covering? Pleasure requires self-discipline and anguish.

Basic proposition: avoid equilibrium.

You see that my silver skull is asymmetrical. Therein lies my productivity. From the ever-changing combinations you lose the unhappy nostalgia for things and the painful attachment to finality. Up to now you haven't dared to think that. The world is the medium of thought. It hasn't got to do with knowing; that is an extravagant tautology. Here it is about thinking, thinking. That, dear sir, changes the whole situation. Geniuses don't act, or only appear to act. Your goal is thought, a new, the newest thought.

Sir, do you now understand the great Napoleon ? The man was not ambitious. That is merely the projection of scheming university dilettantes. That man constantly attempted new ways to think, but he was too much of an ideologue. Grant me one thing, don't weave me in with the unstable emotional gushing of a pantheist. These people have never conceived a good picture image. That is their mistake. They are distracted schoolboys. They cannot advance beyond a concept; that is what I reject. The concept is as much a tautology as the object. You cannot abolish the art of combination. The concept requires things but I want the opposite. I direct my attention to pleasure. Now you know that my end could be described as tragic. Get dressed. We will go and witness a hypothetical action: my funeral wake.'

CHAPTER FOUR

Bebuquin stared for weeks at the corner of his room and wanted the corner of his room to come to life out of himself. It unnerved him to be dependent on the incomprehensible and unending facts which negated him. But his exhausted will couldn't raise a speck, with closed eyes he could see nothing.

'It must be possible, just as in the old days, to believe in a God who created the world out of nothing. How anguishing that I can never be complete. But why do I lack even the illusion of completeness?' Then he thought he still had the capacity to represent the actual within himself. He regretted how everything appeared the same to him. It wasn't the case that the general instinct had perished in him. He told himself that value was alogical, and he didn't want to create logic. He felt no liveliness in this contradiction, only recession, rest. It wasn't the negating which pleased him. He despised such a pretentious nagger. This impurity of dramatic men he held in contempt. Perhaps, he wondered, it was his own laziness that brought him to this consideration. But the reasons were beside the point for him. It was a matter of logical thought and from whence the source came.

Böhm greeted him in an easy and friendly manner. He was relaxing since his death as he knew little for certain about immortality. 'It's pretty decent of you and shows you in a good light how, with your contempt for death, you occupy yourself with logic. Sadly you may not have success since you only grant a logical and a not-logical. My dear friend, there are many logics within us, struggling among themselves and out of whose struggle the alogical emerges. Do not allow yourself to be conned by second-rate philosophers going on about the One and the relationship of all parts to each other and their integration with the whole. We are not so lacking in wit that existence needs to claim a God. All these calls to the concept of unity appeal to the laziness of people. Just look here, Bebuquin; people haven't a notion about the nature of the body. Remember those aureoles around the saints in old pictures. Take this literally. Because all that is clichés. What you lack, my dear, is the miracle. Do you grasp now why you keep avoiding all circumstances and things. You are a phantasist without sufficient means. I also once sought the miracle. Remember Melitta who fell out of the megaphone and how embarrassed I was. One only needs women to make a fool of oneself. That is the principle of natural selection, which is just, for there is nothing in women but stupidity. That is why one talks to her about possibilities, and finally understands that the woman is a figment. I have delved into this since my happy demise. You are a phantasist because you are impotent. The imaginary is as much about matter as form. There is one thing you shouldn't forget. Phantasists are people who can never deal with a triangle. One ought not to say that they are symbolists. For God's sake, you need this dilettantism. Have you never seen a couple, or a leaf. Think of a woman under a street lamp, a nose, a lit-up belly, nothing else. Light caught by houses and people. That would be something to speak of. Keep away from quantitative experiments. In art, number and size are both irrelevant. When they play a part they are certainly subsidiary. Working with infinity is a purer form of dilettantism. I will give you some advice which might be of help to you later. Kant will certainly play a big part. Note this. His seductive meaning is that he created an equilibrium between the object and the subject. But one thing, the main thing he forgot was that which the cognising subject does, namely, constitute a subject and object. Is that the psychic thing-in-itself? There's the nub and why German idealism so completely exaggerates Kant. The uncreative will always exhaust themselves on the impossible. Knowing no limits, or, how much of the spiritual objects can support, for which they are responsible. All this chatter of the infinite comes from formless and unused spiritual energy. As it is, the expression of potential energy is a matter of powerful incapacities.'

CHAPTER FIVE

Around the table the Viennese cane chairs formed a rhythmic garland. The nose of a drunkard abruptly intensified the chain. Lights were hanging lumpily from the ceiling and splattered the wall into tatters. 'So one thing annihilates the other,' remarked the youthful painter Heinrich Lippenknabe.

'I have been trained to find negation everywhere.

Yet, despite that, the most interesting thing is the benevolence of annihilation. The tension in everything is comical. It is a pity that art and philosophy have taken as their task the giving of still form to the ever fragmentary. In our usual energy there has to be the habit of disintegration. In concealing the violent fear of expansion, the energy of form demonstrates the rhythm of tiredness.

I have always concerned myself with seeing everything as temporary. I constantly meet with people who exhibit the symptoms of abandoning strong values, and who, after straying briefly, turn to art and have intrapolated absolutes in the subconscious belief that this is okay, and extrapolate their aesthetic principles into the artistic domain. Soon they forget this and adopt the slack values by which they can live and rest and work in peace. The aesthetic transits to the ethical, principally by a process of exaggeration.

I admitted I was pleased to see that formal art emerged from symbolic art in the case of a talented few, but then perhaps it was the symbol which created the artistic, as the artistic had to overcome the limitlessness of the former, and from this the current split emerged.

Don't you agree that the early Christians think and argue with images, and because of this they were compelled to a great energy of form and to an enduring sensuous variation of quietude within the self.'

Bebuquin said: 'It is the accomplishment of Schopenhauer to have demonstrated quiescence as the essential being of all subjects and things. He restated the platonic unmoved Idea, the fundamental and pristine law; but in fact being is a nothingness. Because of that the reduction to sense impressions is unbearable. With great difficulty I might one day be clearer about productivity. This child-like searching for a beginning will ruin me.'

Euphemia entered the café. The yellow light gave her – as it moved like waves under oars and frothed around her stooks – the same contours that flowed in her hat and splayed out from the long and dangling feather bouquet. She wasn't seen much since she gave birth to a baby boy. It appeared that the birth had been good for her body. Bebuquin thought spontaneously that by getting rid of the fat with the child she had rid herself of all her bad experiences. She really looked like a young virgin.

'How's that for rotten luck that we men come from woman?'

Euphemia: 'Well, young fellow, haven't I recovered brilliantly?'

Heinrich Lippenknabe started up a song whose pale long piccolo was accentuated by the crinkling of curtains and the clinging of the metal curtain rings.

'The stink of loneliness greets us from afar.

> On all our weary travels,
> from a patch of blue our eyes
> suck loneliness.
> It is a dank dark room
> without walls, whose height no man has measured.
> Around us the cosmos dances full of tricks.
> No glimmer falls on me.'

'Would you shut up with that rubbish? I want to concentrate the whole story in myself.'

'You can do that easily; simply believe it.

I have often thought that our opinions could be taken as the complete reversal of the facts.

Negation says nothing, just as little as affirmation. The artistic begins with the word *other*. Artistic forms could have established themselves and gone to such an extent beyond things that they would create an object. The world has become *gehenna* for you and you think it should be sacrificed to the dumb show of the poet. But we are trapped in our memories and depend upon our tautologies – in this I am ignoring the word *form*.

The essence of this word is that it includes everything with the nothing, and by the same token, is more than the concept of the symbol. On the one hand it goes far beyond logic and leaves experience with much more significant signs; it is auto-kinetic: rest and movement are both encompassed in it. The symbol gave us the before and after of form, the empirical and the alien; but form secretes itself between the two elements. Form goes beyond causality also, and has more important traits than the idea; it is more than a process. Above all it can enter into combination with every organ and thing, and since its responsibility to the object is intellectually loose it fulfils it without rape. In it, the Christian denial of form comes to an end, towards which it strives with all the simple and pure powers of the soul. Christ did not even give us an apparent end result: he spasmodically negated and raped. Perhaps form will bring forth new objects; it is further removed from its origins than the concept, and a deduction on the basis of form is to be distinguished from a conceptual one. In it, perception gains a force which was previously uniquely given to the concept.'

CHAPTER SIX

A blue feather of Euphemia's hat drowned itself sparklingly in the green Chartreuse.

Bebuquin goggled with his left leg into the corner of the bar where Heinrich Lippenknabe introspectively arranged an orchid in the bronzed navel of a courtesan and doused it with brandy.

'Who is the father?' the barmaid screamed.

The beam of the electric lamps penetrated through her toes to the knees and danced merrily backwards over the crystal flasks and the coolers; That usually polite electric light!

'No one,' Euphemia stared with her crossed stalked eyes. 'I got him in a dream.'

'Crap,' said Heinrich Lippenknabe, 'she means a useless contraceptive.'

'In the first place I hadn't an idea who the father might he. Sure, it's all the same.' Euphemia looked frightened.

'Maybe it was Böhm?' asked Bebuquin.

Euphemia screamed out directly.

'He is always coming to nurse the baby, and has such a milky skull since he died, he uses his entrails, for which he has no further need, as a zither and sings the theorem of Pythagoras with feeling. He said the kid must become an intellectual.'

'Yes, your embryo wrote a philosophical work, and wasn't he conferred doctor at birth? and isn't the whole story called: The Destroyed Umbilical Cord, or, the principium individuationis?'

'Yes,' Euphemia whispered, 'he has already renounced the world and is becoming holy, completely without desires, dirty and silent. Apart from that he has sensitive skin which changes colour incessantly. Couldn't one use him for advertising signs. It would save on the coloured bulbs.'

'The a-logical grows, the a-logical conquers, it will not let up.'

Bebuquin balanced on a bobbling barstool.

'That is why, ladies, so many go mad. We crave fiction, positivism destroys.'

The barmaid knelt, enraptured among the ice pails.

'O Lord, we conceptualise too materially.'

Her lace dress glittered around her, ornament of dreams.

The coolers, holy vessels of the unspeakable. 'We will make no more sacrifices,' Bebuquin screamed into the street. 'The sublime has got lost. You criticise the miracle: the miracle makes sense only when incarnated, but you have destroyed all the forces that transcend the human.'

'I want the spirit to become visible,' groaned Heinrich Lippenknabe.

'The nothing should materialise itself,' the woman with the orchid in her navel.

Böhm stood among them.

He spoke, saying:

'Natural law ought to be soused in alcohol until it comprehends that there are irrational situations, until it grasps that lawfulness is for the weak voting democrat. Law cannot achieve spiritual realisation. It hangs senselessly on the nail of a bad mathematical axiom.

As soon as something is recognised by the law, that proves the thing is outlived as experience. Law is the past, subjected to death.

Sic.

We lack exceptions.

Too few people have the courage to speak complete rubbish. Frequently repeated nonsense becomes the integrating moment of our thinking. Given a certain *niveau* of intelligence one is hardly at all interested in correctness and reasonableness.

Reason turns too much that is great and sublime into the grotesque and the impossible. With reason we destroyed God, the all-encompassing idiosyncrasy.

What right has reason there? It sits.

On Unity.

There sits the vulgarity.

There are so many worlds which have nothing to do with each other, as little as this green Chartreuse has to do with the visions into which it transforms itself.

When a sympathetic contemporary has something to do with the extraordinary they lock him up in a lunatic asylum.

Gentlemen, that man does not interest himself in your rational world. Why can't you at least realise that your reason is boring?

Reason stylises everything, most of which is dumped cheaply for purportedly trivial transitions; the rest is canonical: the valuable, the boring, the democratic, the enduring.

Gentlemen, the intelligence and imagination of people demonstrates in fact that one can trap lightning, discriminate please. I want to assure you that I am alive, only because I suggest it to myself, in reality I am dead. You already know I allowed myself to be entombed. But I swore to myself that I would walk around as an ensign for unreality until some fool experiences a miracle on account of me. Look, babies, unreal nothing; those are the denominators for your bad eyes. If there is future abundance it comes from the nothingness, the unreal. That is the only guarantee for the future.

The utilitarian and the critic call the imaginary *illusion* and *maya;* the nothing, either *vacuum* or *aether.* There are people who like to stuff everything into their mouths and swallow it or hack it up into a moral. But the nothing is the indifferent precondition of all Being. The nothing is the fundament; but one shouldn't go so far as to believe in Robert Meyer and argue that all existence is only a reduction of the nothingness. Existence in forms is a sofa, a sleeping bag, an awkward as well as boring convention. If one is brave and free towards the multiplicity of life then one sees death as a prejudice, views it as a deficiency of the imagination, and one opts for the imaginative which is the *élan vital* in all possible forms. I concede that reason makes things so much more cosy, it concentrates things, but it also destroys too much and renders things too ridiculous, especially the highest things. One must regard the impossible for so long that it becomes easy. The miracle is a question of training.

Euphemia you need a cult.

The romantic says: See I have imagination and I have reason, I am weird and sometimes utter things that do not exist, as my reason later informs you. When I want to be very poetic I say the whole story dreamed me. But that is my most sublime trick, it cannot be used too often. Then comes the mask and mirrors as romantic machinery. Gentlemen, that is aestheticism. With the romantics one takes one step forward and two backwards. That's a spastic bandage.'

He doused the not yet departed with absinthe.

'That's the mark of a dilettante.'

Bebuquin struck Euphemia on the nose and simultaneously embraced her with passion.

A rain storm pointillated the large sash window.

'We need a great flood.

Until now we have used reason to vulgarise the senses, to simplify and reduce the perceptions. Reason has diminished us *in toto*; it diminishes God to the merely indifferent; let us murder reason, reason has created the shapeless death in which there is nothing left to see. For Dante death was still an occasion for radiance, colour, wealth and desire. Let us take our senses and tear them out of the stupid sleep of platonic ideas, let us observe the moment, which is more distinctive than quiescence, because it differs, has character, no uniformity, but keeps dividing itself front and back with no rest left over.'

The dead Böhm danced delightedly on Euphemia's hat and sank into the buffet; he lay down again in the same vintage brandy he had always loved.

CHAPTER SEVEN

The three globe lamps swayed in the bar. Their rays loosened from the inner light source penetrated like knitting needles.

Böhm climbed out of the brandy and danced behind the crystal flasks of tinted schnapps, softly warbling the cancan of the chameleon's serpentina alcoholica.

The moons of the lamps became gross, their rays feeling up the décolletage of the ladies. They listened to the mild, dry voice of Bebuquin, recounting his last love.

'Farewell to Symmetry.

My last beloved stood in the garden of enticing curves – she's a vase from Cnidus. A rich woman owned her but could not put up with having her around, because she could not bear her curves to be compared with the vase. She clicked her tongue and kept young aesthetic men around her. To show off her culture she always showed the Cnidian vase to the young men. So the young ones craftily compared the vase with the lady. The vase certainly had the form of a svelte woman, and the lady suffered by comparison and didn't profit from her love of art. This vase almost destroyed me, my senses were moodily abstract. For weeks I looked for a woman with the proportions of the vase. Understandably, in vain. Maybe the doll of Euphemia's cheap thrills. But it was all wrong. In my dreams I got into the vase and broke it regularly. The vessel turned me into a classicist, into a symmetrically divided stylist. Then it dawned on me. Symmetry, like the platonic idea, is a dead end. Böhm once said I should amputate one of my legs. That was brutal, but correct. But the matter wasn't dear to me. Symmetry is as boring as mechanics. Eventually I let myself be given the vase. That meant that both I and the lady of the house were served well. After a fairly bad night I broke the pot in two. It was a matter of life and death. Since then I have become a romantic.'

Bebuquin did not see that the courtesan and Euphemia were sitting crouched up under the lamps, drinking liqueurs and staring at the light. Lippenknabe kissed his mistress on the arm. She shrieked and repelled the painter with a long sharp hatpin drawn from the twitching circle of light.

He retreated completely.

The women lay in transports under the hard, stabbing daggers of the globe lamps.

They moaned like animals.

The lamps began to frizzle and sizzle.

Bebuquin flicked off the switch.

The women came to, bewildered.

The painter said jealously:

'Sun worshippers,' and left.

Bebuquin remained with the women. They drank more and the alcohol spoke like God from the mouth of the prophets.

The pallid morning daubed the windows.

It crawled down the walls of the houses.

The three were nervous about separation. One only leaves when completely exhausted.

They huddled together and a cold wet serpent tightened around them.

The terror of the changing colours of passing time dumbfounded them. The night which loved the garish lit faces died in the day. One felt that one must use the night for serious training, for they all wanted to be visionaries and to be completely inhuman. They had become totally exhausted with their bodies and forms, and desperately wanted to distort themselves.

Under the dull sun the pale phantoms went home.

The landscape was drawn on a board; wide overstimulated staring eyes couldn't feel that it was getting brighter and clearer. The electric bulbs and the encroaching darkness still stuck in their optic nerves. Crying, Bebuquin tried to kick the sun in its imaginary stomach. A diamond in Euphemia's décolletage caught the fresh morning light and intensified it. Giorgio, frightened by the dazzle, screamed 'fuck' and visited her apartment. The whore went on alone. She was left standing unused, so she opened her peacock-coloured umbrella, jumped up wildly a few times, and merged with the surface planes of an advertising hoarding, and became an advertisement for the newly-opened singles shebeen 'Essay'.

CHAPTER EIGHT

The actress Fredegonde Perlenblick rode through the rainy, squally night. For her young lovers she had the name Mah; Lou, when she was being demonic, and Bea when she wanted to substitute as family. She drove with two blindingly bright headlights which shot streams of white light into the slippery asphalt, in whose dark puddles the shadows of the last pedestrians swam. Her car horn had definite dramatic force. The chauffeur possessed a dramatic recitation style; the horn had the theatrical R. On the roof of the hood there was a peep-show for the sleepy citizens, exhibiting how the actress Fredegonde Perlenblick stripped, washed, and went to bed. Before dark the written words 'Alone at last?' appeared over the bed. The racing images were subtitled; for example, 'I wear the *ideal* garter belt,' or sometimes with a valuable recommendation. The actress pulled up in front of the bar. She alighted. No one was there yet. There was no response to her first electric look which crisscrossed the local.

She sat herself down and was beautiful just for herself.

Bebuquin crossed the threshold.

'Madame, you are sitting on a hypothesis.'

'Yes, I am like a disguised boy.'

The lady had provoked look number 5. This time she realised that she would have to pitch higher.

'Madame, do you know that you are proving the non-existence of the material for me.'

'O, we can become stylists in the theatre when it is appropriate. I have tried fustian but it is so hard to wear. You either look like a permanent virgin or merely married. There is no in between.'

She heaved her trembling breasts.

It was silent.

The trickster Böhm sprinkled the throat of Fredegonde from his cognac vat. She reacted. Humbly he spoke:

'Madame, would you like a jewel from my head?'

'I have Büchmann and an anthology of poetry. That is enough,' she said with indignation.

'I mean real ones.'

'Previously I had to sit on a hypothesis, and now you want to pass off your immaterial jewels. Sir, pay attention to a woman's intellect.'

'Baby, haven't you ever heard of a *café latte?* Come on. Let's have our modest game of madness.'

'But one has to be natural. I am always so natural.' Now she began to smile.

Böhm nimbly placed a jewel on her neck and spoke with a horror voice.

'Now you are brought into the dreams.

Cockatoo of pain, be gone.'

The arch of the buffet became brightly coloured. Bird eyes stared out, the walls of the bar became feathered, the clipping of wings could be heard, flying higher, wilder into the madness.

The actress cried out:

'Revolving stage! Shakespeare *à la* Reinhardt,' and held her purse tightly.

The wings of the cockatoo filled with people.

Euphemia sat alone above it all with Emil, the phosphorescent embryo, on her lap, and roared:

'Ladies and Gentlemen, today will be black and white.

We will be so manic that afterwards we won't be able to say a word. O, I am only the wax doll of cheap thrills.'

They then saw a chorus line coming out of them; past years danced around them, fought.

'We must come to our senses,' screamed Böhm.

'Children, in heaven there is only beatific vision. We have to see in such a way that all knowledge is contained in it.'

The people in the street stared out in astonishment at the great beast that banked in the air and screamed:

'The live one is coming.'

The bird screeched in red grey:

'I prove that it can be otherwise.'

The people shook with fear that they might not be able to bear it.

Indeed for the most part one is stuck in dilettantish shock.

It ends with a stroke on the plush sofa.

In front, a white porcelain poodle.

He has a red dicky bow.

CHAPTER NINE

But understandably one does not always fly. With the fourth glass of whiskey neat one sits again with difficulty.

Euphemia said:

'Böhm is a buffoon, I don't know if he is alive or dead.'

Three workers stomped into the bar.

The electric lights reminded them of the factory.

They placed their order. One of them reached for a bottle of *Sekt*.

A sensitive waiter remonstrated. He jerked his knee nervously.

His father was a servant in a family restaurant.

'Gentlemen, you don't know the cockatoo of pain. It is not advisable to get langered.'

A red workshirt with a glowing blue head throbbed.

'We're only having a drop.'

Tucked a few bottles under the arm, along with the actress Fredegonde Perlenblick.

'Athlete,' she moaned in rapture.

Euphemia said contemptuously and apodictically:

'Cows masticate over and over, whether it be hay or Shakespeare. Cows adore bulls.'

From the street one could hear the abusive tragedian.

'Explosive soul.'

She lifted her skirts very high.

Her car sped off greedily.

It cruised along the asphalt, slid across the reflections of the gas lamp and the last dawdler.

Now, d'Annunzio may write this out further.

In the bar they sang the melody of the atheists, to fortify and strengthen Böhm's corpse. Lippenknabe tasted the lilting melody which was like castor oil on his tongue.

'Böhm is destroying all our feeling for form. The old codger is still dead, even if he does flunk around here, fibbing.'

The opening of the debate was interrupted. In came a woman, and close behind her, a worn-out, almost transparent man.

He faced into a corner and chanted.

'Ehmke Laurenz, Platonist, goes out at night, for only then are there no colours. I seek the pure quiescent lonely idea: this lady, energetic rhythmic excitement. I am unique because I am destroyed by two things: the loftiness of the idea, and the debasement of the lady.'

'Yes, but why not destroy both of them, as they entail each other, or, at least your nonsensical ideology of being, of *ennui,* of death. That is just fatigue, a defect; Platonism is anaesthesia. Pluck out your eyes and your ears: then you'll bring your Platonism back on track.'

Aurora, the wife of the rum customer, who principally drank colourless schnapps, approached and said:

'Ehmke makes you consider things.' He looked at her pleadingly and then said with contempt: 'You don't know me' – 'Then you know me better,' she said. He grinned like a little fool, sunk his head to his navel; his face drained of colour and he looked vacantly at his stomach.

Meanwhile she was very affectionate.

In the end they became such nuisances they had to be thrown out; nothing is so excessive and boring as an ideologue and a whore: they both have the most banal form of spleen.

After a short time a stranger came in and like everyone blended in with his tailcoat.

Meanwhile Böhm slithered out of his brandy and shouted:
'That's him.'

Euphemia went to the unknown one as if in a trance and
said: 'You are a complete stranger to us, but horribly distinctive,
I am obliged to give myself to you.'

The stranger said in a normal voice:

'Please come with me.'

'And why shouldn't we love God,' Bebuquin said gently.

'Because the unknown is the treasure of the seeking creator,'
whispered Lippenknabe.

The clock ticked the seconds; every second was three-
dimensional, distinct, the eye saw the sound. For a moment
the earth was a crystal fire, and people transparent glass.

Bebuquin sighed. Against the windowpanes, from the
colourful morning wind, the beginning of rain.

CHAPTER TEN

People ignorant of each other traipsed in spoonfuls into the
circus, a colossal rotunda of amazement, sat packed together
and waited for Miss Euphemia. The ornaments of excited
hands ran along the railings, and the globe lamps swung their
milk buckets.

Miss Euphemia was first noticed when she was hoisted up
to the top; she supported herself with her teeth on a tightrope.

She released herself and made a *salto mortale* right across
the top from one end to the other, where with her teeth she
tore into another tightrope.

A programme fell.

Miss Euphemia slid off the rope a third time: she had decided for formal reasons to break her neck.

People screamed; some tried to jump out of the galleries. Euphemia saw the swinging chandelier and five and a half metres from the ground she grabbed the tightrope.

The audience convulsed with rage.

With great confidence, Euphemia then executed some more somersaults.

In spite of this she was morally ruined.

(The strongest morality, that of the hand crafts.)

She thought it fitting to enter a convent and repent.

People drifted into the cool evening, dispersed and disappeared.

The circus was empty, a rounded darkness.

In front of a sleeping monkey cage, Euphemia whipped herself.

CHAPTER ELEVEN

The shadow of a pair of copulating monkeys crept over Euphemia from the other side of the cage. She quivered with tiredness from the tenebrous lust that crawled over her. She went quietly to the middle of the arena, took off her gauze dress and stood nude in the darkness. A few faint stars shone through the skylights. The fatal rope swung between them.

'You are done for,' Bebuquin cried through the gloom. His shadow slid across the floor and over Euphemia.

'Don't lay a hand on me,' she cried. 'I belong to the other. I have promised myself to the imagined Böhm. He could emerge from the wall. He is beyond every rule. He has muddled up everything for me. His macabre and formless humour which makes everything meaningful and meaningless has got to me. I suffer so much from the temptation of the imagination. A woman cannot endure this. Look, Böhm is much more real for me than you. He is a mordant wit, a fantastic guillotine. O, you, my gallows. I always look the way he wants me to look. He extracts all the strength from my limbs. I squat for days and see him in the evening shadows, then fresh in the morning like a ceaseless cockatoo, or he floats in the sea and for days I follow after the wave and the green bottle that envelops him. It is so enriching to be associated with the dead. It is a tranquil, inner, probing lust, a silent exploding frenzy; Böhm!'

'Your tropes are confused.'

'O you are silly, I am in a long old myth that has enmeshed me like a web. You know the air is completely different, it is a glass bell. I must escape. One chokes miserably in this confined life. With persistent training Böhm expanded the fantastic capacities of his own body, his voice, the rays of his eyes. Yes, it was amazing how far they could reach. I am simply lost in the limitlessness of his humour. But I suffer from all this misery. With a benign smile I could kill anyone; that might lift the burden. Finally, you know, we always act out of a modicum of stress that we discover to be released from it. A total and a less complete darkness, an ounce from being overwrought. Evil and goodness is tempered in us, they weaken each other. But if something within us becomes very tense – hatred, fear, love –, then quick as lightning it covers the whole distance; or else we are somnambulists, who have forgotten all other sensations, do the necessary and are what we were previously, knowing nothing. This is how murder comes about.'

'But the body, the senses.'

'O, my God, they are the poorest habits, prejudices. The feelings which need no experience are far more attractive, stronger and dangerous. Finally, there are people who come on earth and know everything. Life is just an arduous enactment of memory, nothing new.'

'Then we do come from God.'

'Where else?'

'But you produced Emil.'

'No, that wasn't me but something in me producing and supporting. And the first cry of the child, that couldn't have come from me. The form, the body is only a means of expression and a poor instrument. When I am more with God and Böhm I will know the rest of it a lot better.'

'Thus goes everything from the living to the dead. They stand guard with energy. You know, Euphemia, how easily you slipped out of your panties? Everything is slipping from me in the same way. You just stand straight, your head above the clouds, and you are more or less ready. It all falls away. People, whims, troubles, and you are just like an empty cardboard box. As you well know, darkness, the sun are not contraries for me, they are a non-feeling, sometimes in black, sometimes in white. I want to scream out once so that tigers break out in fear and their eyes shine through the night. Nothing would give me greater pleasure. Nothing. Everything that thrills other people and makes them ecstatic bores me to death and makes me as still as the wall you can't see. And now you turn to the Lord God! You might just as well hang yourself in perpetuity. The Lord God, that's it. We give him all our force and then can't stand him any longer. I see how everything falls to him, how he takes you from me. Then there is nothing else

I can do, I grant him no rights, and I can't die just because you believe in an extraterrestrial being.'

'Giorgio, do you know what a pure woman is? Do you know that women of any worth for the most part despise themselves. I want to get out of all this shit.'

Bebuquin: 'Into your grey leaden sour milk days.'

Euphemia: 'Into a quickening of the soul.'

Bebuquin: 'God is madness.'

Euphemia: 'Thereby more of a stronghold.

    Just like inhuman mathematics, luxurious and passionate.

    God is the excitement that transcends the body.

    God is the death that we die beyond ourselves.

    He is the fecund annihilation of ourselves.

    He is immeasurable measure.

    Unseen colours.

    O how shall I dance him.

    I will have to gather up the stars in my hands.

    Lay the sun down under my soles.

    That my mouth may be a limitless orchestra.

    And the brass and the bass drum completely busy.

    I crush grapes in my fingers.

    And know him.

    I lie still and am white as plaster that covers the wall, and know God.

    He is the glimmering lurker in the dark.'

Bebuquin: 'He is insanity.

    The impossible one.

    The deathly undoing.

    The infertile steppes into which we compel our dwellings.

Mortal danger for the will.

He is my hate.'

'Bebuquin, let's catch our breath. You are a selfish man, you make no sacrifices, you want everything for yourself, and that just won't do. Leave something, and not too little, for the Lord God. O, isn't that Böhm?'

She became cold, then a hot sweat broke out over her body.

'Listen,' said Giorgio, 'that is nonsense. It is simply awful to think that everything is seduction and temptation. Euphemia, marry me, otherwise it is not to be endured.'

'Yes, and Böhm watching us every night. Do you have no *pietas*?'

'If only something would possess me enough that I could be released from myself, a sympathetic suicide. Do you think it's fun running around with myself the whole time, and I don't have the desire or the talent to be the full Goethe.'

'Giorgio, do you believe that someone like you would arouse a woman one inch out of the saddle. As soon as you say something, it goes against you. I don't trust myself to speak against your will in saying: you behaviourist pet.'

This she spoke without self-interest. Fourteen days earlier she would have said it with gusto. For the Lord God demands his rights, and one rises up only to fall.

Poor Bebuquin. You tamed beast.

With a dying fall religiousness sounds erotic in front of a monkey cage.

Bebuquin meandered along the physiology of the houses with a sore throat. A prostitute danced tipsily at the street corner and mooned her corseted and padded bottom to the starry skies. Don't tell me how Bebuquin must obliterate the great delight with drugs. Euphemia calmly and sanctimoniously donned a nun's habit and left the circus. Earnest, polishing her fingernails, shaking her head, now and again testing the firmness of her breast, she casually entered the convent of the gratuitous Miracle of the Blood.

CHAPTER TWELVE

Bebuquin went unnoticed into his apartment. After bathing he dressed himself carefully. Then, isolated from puzzles, he went into his cathartic closet, a little whitewashed room with an easy chair in the middle.

He sat down humbly and said:

'O delight of sin.

But not for dishonourable motives. It uplifts and makes strong. Sin requires that we forget everything that happened up to then and start all over again. Sin is a death and my world is consumed in it. Up to now so many Bebuquins have descended into hell, and it compels me again and again to be purer and stronger, despite my diminished powers. Perhaps one sins only to obtain the purity of repentance, renewal through parsimony.

Still the pain.

When I think of sin, I can't go on living. When I forget it, my life disappears with this word, and I surrender it to Satan.

God, when can I give you my life's end?

O, just to start to do without an old and marked body, in order to experience identity.

This night a friend of mine died.

My thoughts were wiped out.

Eyes and ears are sinful.

What remains apart from philosophy;
I am condemned without principles
always to be evil.
Does my meanness need such switches?'

He went silent. A cave stuck in him and around him the ground was cut away. The line was broken. His eyes lay unmoving above his cheekbone.

He spoke:
'O Kingdom of my soul,
Perhaps also of helpless multiplicity,
that it cannot bear.
Then this poverty.
It wracks me.
When will it understand
that in order to live,
to be a person,

one may only know one thing. O, to feel the delight of the manifold of words and meanings; and how painful to learn only one interpretation. Form makes things, the stiff eyes, the steady tone. If only I could hide myself in the *jouissance* of the multiple and not know from what centre I would resurrect.

Lord, you gave us work: spare me from it so that I can intuit the possible immensity rather than achieve a minimum. What a foolish suggestion, this word. So I lie with ears alert, like a colourful animal on your ground, awaiting a message; for today I have no shroud in which I could rise from the dead.

O God, you gave us a body, maybe identical; a soul which transcends the body's possibilities, which long and often has been able to discard it; and the shining bald head of the thinkers – in which the sun deigns not to reflect itself –

searching for balance. But I will that my spirit wants to think itself other than this body – O garden fences, city walls and safes, boarding schools and hymens – to think itself and create something new. I can make strange beings, crazy drawings on paper with words. I myself am distorted; but my stomach remains a guzzler. What a narrow pursuit of the saints, to try and change the body from some saying of the gospels.

O Lord, grant me a miracle; we have been seeking it since chapter one.

Then I will be normal, but only then.

O God, if you are more than the law of researchers approximating truth, have mercy on my boredom; Böhm has already died from it.'

'Bebuquin,' it was said, 'the whole thing is a reformatory. Those beyond are so humanly simple. There are two possibilities, either they are silent and make an imaginary phallus infinite, or they achieve the same thing by drawing the number 1. I draw 1's and my isolated skull rusts. I greet you, old martyr. Destroy identity and you will fly rapidly; but it is doubtful if you will withstand the tempo. One, Hallelujah, one, Hallelujah, Amen, one. O necessity, Hallelujah, O law, O unity, where all sleeps in itself, O silence, O contemplation, O digestion of ostriches that eat their own droppings.

One, Hallelujah, one, Hallelujah, have a nice day, one, hallel–'

Was that philosophy or an illiterate?

'O equality, O one. Some still count up to two. O expansion of dualism. O going between the shores, O running back and running forth.'

Ancientness of thoughts, O antiquaries of the commonplace, O prehistoric profundity.

'Look, my life is hateful to me, it is absolutely destroyed. To carry on normally, I need new conditions for existence, more than bread. I can't continue in chains; don't want that, it would be morally trivial. Don't drive me into the old tracks by being forgiving; a change must come which is stronger than my sin and my repentance. I must have a renewal. I need an apocalypse.'

The night colours slowly, the white room opalised like an old jewel, licking shadows crawled along the wall. A small white cloud hung outside the window, glowing from the sunburst that illuminated it. Bebuquin's body disappeared in the shadows with just the head staring at the sinking cloud, the head the colour of twilight. His head, a cooling star.

CHAPTER THIRTEEN

Once again the stars compete in vain with the definite light of the arc lamps.

'O art,' sighed Bebuquin, 'you are powerful when one elaborates the perspectival, the desired changes of conditions, how a thing can be simultaneously true and false, depending on the point of view.

Temptation, you emerge from the decimated sleeping night and increase yourself because of our fear of the stars.

I have not forgotten, in so far as it is fitting, that perhaps another will purify me when I am not able to do so.'

So he entered the cloister of the gratuitous Miracle of the Blood, wondering if a complete rupture of destiny was possible.

Above him, on the needles of the pine tree, Böhm slid along.

He sang:

'O woods, with your fond embroidery,

O terror, sage of secrets.

Forest fires, your revelation in the bush.

Labyrinths, obstacle paths,

    meandering driven soul who traipses there.'

His skull lit the path with the nonchalant certainty of the dead. He sang on:

'Risks, speculations of the weak

which are empty,

for paperweights are being pressed.

O philosophical subterfuges.

The fine innocent soul of a naïve child

roams in the forest.'

Lightning struck the forest, the tree above which Böhm was rising, trembled.

Bebuquin had enormous trouble keeping abreast of Böhm's aerial voyage, despite the fact that he was really respectful; but often when Böhm intended things to be going swimmingly, Bebuquin was sinking into the morass, or as he climbed breathlessly out of it, Böhm danced too nimbly over the tip of an acacia.

'O viewpoints, multiplicity of the logician, the counterpoint of spheres,' shouted Böhm, carefully protecting the silent light of his lamp, 'you who mangle things up, but can hardly destroy them.

How you thrill my eyes,

for I have weaned myself from fatidic thinking.

Bebuquin, the will to stupidity demands renunciation, and that you achieve by thinking things through carefully. Then you see that our thoughts collapse in upon themselves like the wings of a wild hen that has been shot. Thoughts are not goals in themselves, they have value as movement; but can thoughts move; o, they fix exactly, they nail tightly, they even conserve the revolutionary. Images are the deeds of the eyes, though not everything is said with a picture; but a thought pretends otherwise, it has exhausted the whole and paralyses.

Logic always wants completeness and does not realise there are many kinds of logic. There is no primordial one, although there is a tendency to unification, and many things repel each other. Logic does not have a single foundation. Of its four axioms, some love this one, and some love the others; and an axiom struggles and mixes with the others, for one axiom by itself cannot take a step forward. Logic is monstrous exception, and the theorem of Pythagoras, a chimera.'

Green dragons with droning metallic tails flew across the sky. Dust rose against the sky from the desert across which Bebuquin dragged himself.

The cloister stood at the horizon; around it lay the sterile, stylising, droning desert, overflown with birds, the visual plane where the view circles round and turns in on itself and collapses in the sand; and the sun beat down on this brown skin with crashing strokes of light above the fanfare of jagged cliffs.

CHAPTER FOURTEEN

A man sat in front of the cloister looking into himself. In an attempt to show what could be achieved here, although only granting a slight foretaste, a woman floated above him. It was the Platonic couple. He curved himself by hugging his head with his feet; and she circled, revolving within herself, above his white close-cropped skull.

They chanted quietly.

'Silence of those sunken into themselves, consecrated and gyrating around themselves. When will everything cohere in itself for us? Many paths join in this rapturous insight, the idea as well as the whorish, blistered feet and dead contempt, childish imprudent business with ultimate concepts. O infamous infinity of the lazy, the tired, the shirkers, whores and bastards, whom you will certainly ruin, you who destroy form and active force. O vile sinking into the point of points, into the A O, into the fundament, into the resolution.'

Bebuquin passed them by and went into the ecstatic outer courtyard. It was always the same. The ecstasy was aroused and heightened by a nothing, a quarry of black marble, across which one could float, into which one could stare, in which to be silent, because of which one was aroused, in which everything petrified, where one could shout, above which one could dance, scourge oneself, and so on. Others had instead of that a crystal rock and in long speeches recommended its bright transparency, its fire, its power of perspective, its facets, its creative three-dimensionality, its form, its composure, its purity, and so on. Many people worked around the stone, rolling it near the black quarry, turning it upside-down above it, holding it, lowering it into the quarry almost to the floor. The distortions caused by its facets made it impossible to judge whether it fit the quarry or not. On top of this a committee of hypotheses was formed, while vulgar opponents with large noses demanded that its fit be determined by smell, that the bowel movements be sniffed and measured aerostatically, and the curve through which their excrement passed to the earth be measured ballistically. An apparently exclusive group of postulants played with a mask and a mirror, but about that one ought not to speak. From a small colonnade came the monotone voice of a bonze.

'I and Thou are one; this identity holds the world together. Contemplation is an imaginative capacity, for it reaches beyond things into spiritual community. It is a more fundamental feeling than the law of contradiction. In my luminous love, B equals A. Ground and goal are one. Each turns into the other again, in order to find itself. O equality of force, O not-happening, O events, most high and univocal.'

Bebuquin screamed: 'You are creating justified suicide here, sacred stupidity is being bred, eyes are being torn out. Sir, I came here in order to fabricate a new human being. I live from another word. I cannot use your unity.'

The bonze replied to him:

'Let your appearance be other. Anyway it is irrelevant what you think. You are only the primordial ground and therefore without sin in your deepest interior.'

Bebuquin swore.

'I am not in the least interested in the primordial ground. I despise it.'

Böhm approached in yellow monk's-robes.

'One hope remains, Bebuquin. Perhaps metamorphosis comes with death. Either we remain there as what we are or we will be annihilated and transformed.'

Bebuquin: 'But isn't it possible that one can transform oneself in life, that one can lose one's wretched memory?'

'Bebuquin you have made yourself sick. Sin does not consist only in memory but also in the deed that haunts men and heaven.'

'So one must die in order to become different?'

'Confess and make a sacrifice. I thought the imagination sufficient; I was duped. Go, and make a clean breast of it.'

Bebuquin shouted confessionally through the door of the chapel:

'I renounce being reduced and emptied by purification. I disapprove of beginning in kenosis. I want another destiny; I've seen my fate, and it is nothing but the repetition of a stupidity. I beg that, from among the many things I can imagine to myself, it will be granted to me to become one of them.'

The confessor retorted from within the chapel:

'You imagine many things to yourself but the only representations which have any meaning are the ones you can deal with. You need the fundamental metamorphosis, but that is death.'

Bebuquin: 'Many things occur which cannot be classified, which are ignored or rejected, that are hidden from deadly reason.'

Strophe: 'The withered trees of my garden reflect themselves in the blind crystal ground;

The movement of my hands ends in stillness;

all burning, flying, tearing

will be petrified.

The days join themselves to the slumbering mountain;

and the more dead, the more binding,

imperishable, steeper,

insurmountable, what remains, holding me back,

the past.'

Antiphon: 'The capable change their past in their changing present and future, and thus transform themselves, acquire meaning, and whether sterile or dangerous, by the tenth year happiness is the only solution.'

Strophe: 'What remains in memory is the lost force and constraint, binding one to the same sins. What has been works like a stencil; we stand in the flow, the same water constantly boiling.'

So they bantered on further. Bebuquin opined:

'You see, logic paralyses in so far as our capacities direct themselves towards so-called facts. It only considers our practical requirements, it directs itself towards things and seeks to hold these in a coherent and repetitive relationship. But in my own self the most valuable part transcends such facts. The material world and our imagination can never be congruent. That is why action is so necessary, this corrective of things and facts. But if one arrives at the conviction, as one has, that we must go further, is it not then possible that a new kind of human being will arise who would be ashamed to walk down the same street?'

Trumpets and drums sounded from the roof of the chapel. Bebuquin entered. He spoke further:

'Up to now the religious became grotesque because of facts, or vice versa. Maybe these things can never be joined, so that the creative never ceases. God is the phantastic, of which the entire suppressed and speechless sensibility wants to speak, we baulk against the continuing same choices; the world must transform itself for us.'

CHAPTER FIFTEEN

It is suggested that on the following night Bebuquin spoke at length and coherently. He said into the emptiness of the room:

'I begin the speech about life and death, of the great repose, of holy poverty, and empty purity.

One thing goes through life and that is you, the all too frequent word *No*. But another remains and is very respected, O repose.

I know you are as seductive as the depths of water for young girls, printed in the morning under Miscellaneous.

You are certainly the mother of perfection and the father of metaphysics, for in repose there is *techné* and the enduring end,

there is only isolation, undiluted.

But it stands and curses you,

the weariness that paralyses my thoughts and eyes,

which has clogged my swift feet.

O, you tired brain and sluggish blood,

indifferent even to awaiting death.

But he is inextricably entwined in life,

and every day of toil and growth is a daily death.

And of the two which is right? I think both are one and the same and that life cancels itself out.

O dead life!

The Platonist, he thinks, disputes and his difficult goal is certainty and rest.

Make power and undo it.

Who knows if the discovered idea enables more than it initiates.

Perhaps it strengthens you, most primitive sureness: spirit, I will not bow to you;

Thus he teaches the fool to reject a hundred things for your sake.

And I saw that man is only a vortex from which things flow out of and others go in, until you, O repose, come.

O purity, what else can you say but that you can only bear a little.

The teaching of holy poverty is the same.

You have been such high forms of knowledge.

Death and infinity, you are the inspiration of our work, you push us to effort; and perhaps you are the father of life, and this comes from you but meanly.

You cause the stars to shine and show us our slight strength; as sun and moon shine to each other in a necessary embrace. We can only orient ourselves by one star, for to our eyes they are excluding contraries.

Death, you are the father of procreation, and you give to us humans a sense of finality, verifying our senses, what forms can be seen, heard, tasted, and affirm the hunch of our perhaps dilettantish spirits, and thereby we can see and regard one thing – and thinking that, we see nothing.

I am an executor for you, death. I state it, that only the dying die; when one who is young and strong dies, perhaps he dies for another.

You give us desires and purposes, and we protect ourselves against you with the timeless, with existential ideas, with our claim to totality. But these perhaps are your lowest forms.

Death, father of the comic, if only a miracle that I see with my eyes would destroy you.

Your enemy is the imagination that is beyond rules.

But art makes it immobile and, exhausted, it takes forms.

I name you, death, father of intensity, the lord of form.
That's how things stand for this life.'

Night entered the room.

An old man came into the room, he spoke:

'Excuse me, I have lived for a long time below you, I have great difficulty in speaking as I have not been used to doing so for long.

I come only to sit, on account of my will I have been dead a long time; I only seem to live; be so kind as to substantiate that I have got around death. I die as the greatest humourist.'

The old gentleman collapsed and was silent and stiff. He then cried out loudly and said:

'That was even worse, it deceived only life and myself.'

Bebuquin carried the corpse into the old man's apartment. He looked around for a long time and then went back to his own place.

He stared out the window at the broad tree-lined avenue below. Some people came drifting by and screamed:

'Law is the murderous exception, we go into things in order to seek the miracle.'

Bebuquin turned from the window, the moon shone an astonished hole in his back; he sat himself down, looked at his hands, which had never worked, and declaimed.

'From what are you woven, indifference; was too great a sensitivity your progenitor, or was it the force which is equal to that of opulent nature? I have seen many commit the most whimsical caprices out of indifference, and some out of fear of their own violent anger. O paralysis, stagnating death, petrification and sleep: you conserve life which, were it not for your restraining influence, would consume itself with violent rage.

O sickness come, only you can give me boundaries. God, let me experience searing pain, so that the spirit may be paralysed; or perhaps, O hope, that sickness may create a new body capable of the special things that I need.

Lord, it knows at the end of a thing its most intense degree is not to be found, but its opposite, and that knowledge becomes insanity. I was made to know and see, but your world was not intended for that; it leaves us, abandons us. Seeking you, O Lord, means that we die in speechless paralysis, and it is no revelation; for you are the end.

Lord, let me say one thing:

I have created from myself.

Look at me, I am an end in myself; allow me an independent deed, allow me to perform a miracle.

O night of transformation, when will you come, where I can forget this body, yes, cast it off, and things may mean something else, different from before, and links may become self sufficient, parts begin to speak. Dissolution is transformation: may it be my beginning.'

CHAPTER SIXTEEN

Bebuquin stepped out stiffly into the foggy night. The reflections of the arc lamps blasted through the tree branches and swam like enormous opalescent fish in the wet ground. Bebuquin stood! He ran, and raced through a procession of some new sect; past various messiahs, and some decorative young maidens; It was essential that he get to the circus. He must force expressions of artificial and illogical notions out of himself, so he could finally refute physics with his dying breath.

He went into one of the circus stalls.

Something very particular happened.

During a bicycle trick one of the mirroring columns moved into the arena, sparkling; a flautist walked alongside in the habit of a nun. The audience could see themselves in it, sometimes very large, sometimes distorted; these mirrors compelled one to look into them again and again. Mouths swallowed up the arena and the blackness of the gaping jaws darkened it. Gazes tried to break through the high mirror column. A woman with billowing skirts collapsed under the pressure of avaricious amazement. A gallery fell down. Meanwhile the exactness of the tireless fingers of the flautist and the mirror began a dance with their shadows and those of the audience. These became so worn and confused a woman died: she had lost so much of her shape in the mirror with which the shadows of the others were volubly dancing. The column slipped into the shadows with winging steps.

The people transformed themselves into peculiar signs in the mirror; the public became quietly insane and directed their dizzy contortions to match those of the mirror. Around the mirror colourful reflectors spun.

A recessive darkness, a lightning bolt, driven back into the wall, a number sprung from the gallery.

A young man shot up through the ceiling into the open outside.

'Rabble,' he screamed.

The public broke up further and took the distortions for the real.

Until the empty early morning.

Paralysis entered the city.

Several train carriages halted at midday in front of the circus.

In peaceful sunshine the sorting of the dead was carried out. Then the insane were loaded on.

In the city there was half a year of carnival. The citizens achieved magnificent examples of absurdity. Grotesque convulsions overcame the majority. Cracking each other's skulls became a trivial pursuit. The collective frenzy became so intense that they began to kill.

They started with an old man who was dressed up as Pierrot; he was hanged by the feet from a street sign.

A young girl who still had some critical faculty left screamed: 'Here dies Everyman,' and she beseeched to be hanged as well, for thanks to her ethical sensitivity she was both murderer and victim already.

She was subjected to non-trivial tortures and hanged by the legs. She was abused by everyone for not wearing good underwear. Various messiahs met with success: the messiah of purity, of sex, of the vegetarian, of dance, and the mesmeric messiah, and some others. If you had enough disciples then it became boring. Retired messiahs were employed as newspaper editors, especially if familiar with sensationalism. The new worldview crystallised into a goat with a broken leg.

Several lunatics appeared under Bebuquin's window. He leaned out, his bald head illuminated by the midday sun. The head-bangers bounced up to the windows like balls of rubber; one of them screamed: 'Return us, let us out, take the mirrors away'; for still the glimmering terror of the mirror hung over the city.

CHAPTER SEVENTEEN

Euphemia visited Bebuquin. She knocked on the door. The greeting was like the knocking of bones.

He called out from within, 'Not here, he has been mislaid.'

She entered.

'Euphemia, the connected is falling apart, I explode in a raging self loss.

I was as tight and compact as a Florett foil with its many curves. One becomes simple and blunted.

O forked lightning bolt, O still enduring miserable lamp.

I should have impaled myself upon my own knitting needle, driving it into myself until the shining points sprayed from my brain, flashing, and the skull burst.

One must have the courage of one's madness unto death, and the courage to carry it out.

People who are created for madness struggle with normal women, those child-bearing banalities.'

Standing on her thick legs, smiling sweetly with the insipidity of motherhood, Euphemia said murderously:

'You have no goodness in you.'

He: 'It destroys me. Who will let me be what I must be?'

She: 'You have to be such as allows you to take responsibility of children.'

'But with me is the end of the line.'

Stupid, long, dumb and yawning shadows closed in on him.

'Death,' she screamed.

'Excuse me, two times two is perhaps always four, then it goes on, maybe not, then it is the end.'

She: 'Number is not a fact; it is only a notion of order, and stands outside the soul.'

Car-lights flitted through the room.

'Tear me away from this,' he screamed. There used to be walls here and cut glass windows.

'You defend yourself against yourself and don't have any courage. Which of the two is he? One of them is loathsome to me, disgusting; the other horrible, head over heels in madness.'

Böhm spread himself along the ceiling. A broad shadow with flecks of light, his eyes piercing candles, he swelled when speaking, like a sound-filled sail.

'You two should copulate: discussing nothing better than the self-evident! Or take a cut-throat razor.'

'Böhm, I am growing erect in you. What is this all about?'

He rolled out through the upper chink in the window and climbed carefully into the reflected light beam of a lantern, crying from the element 'Oho!'

Bebuquin said:

'I couldn't have put up with myself or the world without vice, not without will against myself, nor without partial suicide. It is as essential as the so-called positive. Otherwise everything would be spirit, capricious and infinite. In the end it all boils down to the same old opera.'

Euphemia: 'Bebuquin, I never got what I deserved from you. We lay together, you come out with talk of philosophy, that is really comic. One cannot take oneself seriously with you, one contradiction swallows up another.'

Heinrich Lippenknabe entered.

'Ah, there couldn't be a greater contrast. But it should be subject to law. Law is freedom and it transforms contrast into harmony.'

A fat lady swept in, led by her nose.

'One must take pleasure in harmony, resolve everything into *jouissance,* into a blissful state. If you were as fulfilled as I am …'

Bebuquin threw the lady out of the window. Lippenknabe jumps out after her, hits the ground before her, both fall into a wash tub; before they climb out he sells her a painting, they bargain with the water running from them like a fountain under an antique sky.

Bebuquin spoke quietly to Euphemia:

'Everything hangs on death. If it is the end that is all there is, we can never be fulfilled. Does it depend on more than the individual human, and if so is life nothing more than a hindrance. To be on this earth with a purpose is laughable.

Goals are always transcendent, beyond, so we need a beyond, but don't believe it, for every beyond is a thief of power. There are only two methods: either you believe and are with God, you are a mystic and nailed down by an idée fixe; or, you explode and are blown up. Insanity is always the only conceivable result.'

Euphemia: 'Why?'

'These whims that go through me like trams, that tear me away from myself: I am surrounded by this pandemonium of trivialities.'

Below, the confused enthusiasts shuffled on. The painter preached to the fat lady about abstinence, heroic loneliness and the tragedy of being creative, so that she would harmonise with him.

O you viscous voices of the night, haunting the mist-breathing alley, cornerstone of poetic volumes, walks with ones gaze lost in the far away; tottering across piazzas you make light of the long since faded play of children.

CHAPTER EIGHTEEN

'We have to bury Böhm,' cried Bebuquin, 'the codger is becoming a nuisance.'

With respect to the corpse of the deceased an official matter, no one bothered about it; they only wanted to be rid of it.

Bebuquin climbed out of the bar convinced of the possibility of a burial.

The corpse of some suicide was paraded by, behind which was a grieving, empty hearse.

Bebuquin boarded and mumbled on. They came to the city boundary where the last house tried to accentuate the plain without success, and stopped at the cemetery.

Bebuquin sneaked in unseen.

He found an unused plot but hesitated to open a grave there. Then he went at it with a violent rage. By the time he had managed a kind of hole the official obsequies were over. He dug further and stood himself as a cenotaph at the head of the pit, repeating the following epitaph:

'Weep within and be bowed down!'

and crossed his hands upon his breast.

The sun rose and shone upon the one who stood there as the crucified.

Gradually the pose turned into a well-regulated free movement.

'Immateriality, immateriality,' he snarled, and took himself to the grave of a certain Josefine Peters, *née* Dewitz, to shed passionate tears.

CHAPTER NINETEEN

Report of the last three nights.

First night. – Bebuquin lay quietly among the white pillows, stretched out, for some time staring at a hole in the ceiling which didn't stir itself. For a brief moment he thought he was swimming in slimy muck; then he became feverish, and grabbed his head with his fingers, hiding himself anxiously from the open window. He was not capable of speech. After an hour he spoke with full control.

Second night. – Bebuquin resisted going to sleep. It might be dangerous, he thought he would become too caught up in dreams. He speaks with great agitation and senses that dark birds hover over him. The jaws lock.

Third night. – Bebuquin goes to sleep peacefully. His hands jerked up a few times during his sleep, his face gradually got cramped, the skin folded and wrinkled around the whole skull. His eyelids opened in fits and starts every few seconds, he stretched his fingers and spread his toes, then he contracted and trembled convulsively. Toward morning he awoke, but was incapable of speaking and couldn't eat alone any more. Just once he looked coolly and said

Out.

CARL EINSTEIN / BEBUQUIN ODER
DIE DILETTANTEN DES WUNDERS

Ein Roman / Erschienen im Verlag
der Wochenschrift DIE AKTION
Berlin = Wilmersdorf : Dezember 1912

The first edition of *Bebuquin*, published by Die Aktion Verlag in 1912.

Carl Einstein portrayed by Max Oppenheimer, from *Die Aktion*, nr 32 (7 August 1912).

Carl Einstein portrayed by Ludwig
Meidner, 1913.

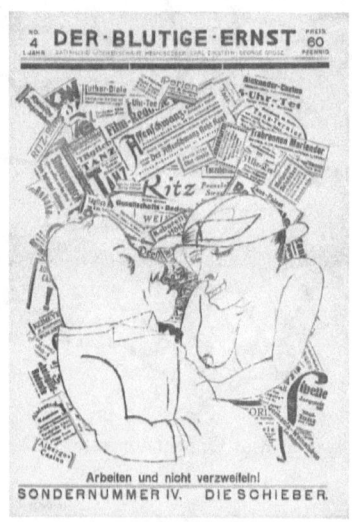

The journal *Der blutige Ernst*, edited
by Carl Einstein and George Grosz,
December 1919.

BEBUQUIN

(GERMAN TEXT)

Für André Gide
Geschrieben 1906/9

ERSTES KAPITEL

Die Scherben eines gläsernen, gelben Lampions klirrten auf die Stimme eines Frauenzimmers: »wollen Sie den Geist Ihrer Mutter sehen?« Das haltlose Licht tropfte auf die zartmarkierte Glatze eines jungen Mannes, der ängstlich abbog, um allen Überlegungen über die Zusammensetzung seiner Person vorzubeugen. Er wandte sich ab von der Bude der verzerrenden Spiegel, die mehr zu Betrachtungen anregen als die Worte von fünfzehn Professoren. Er wandte sich ab vom Zirkus zur aufgehobenen Schwerkraft, wiewohl er lächelnd einsah, dass er damit die Lösung seines Lebens versäumte. Das Theater zur stummen Ekstase mied er mit stolz geneigtem Haupt: alle Ekstase ist unanständig, Ekstase blamiert unser Können, und ging schauernd in das Museum zur billigen Erstarrnis, an dessen Kasse eine breite verschwimmende Dame nackt sass. Sie war so breit, dass sie nicht etwa auf einem Stuhl sass, sondern auf ihrem schwermütigen, weit ausgedehnten Posterieur. Sie trug einen ausladenden gelben Federhut, smaragdfarbene Strümpfe, deren Bänder bis zu den Achselhöhlen reichten und den Körper mit nicht zu aufregend vibrierenden Arabesken schmückten. Von ihren Seehundhänden starrten rote Rubinen senkrecht: »Guten Abend, Herr Bebuquin«, sagte sie. Bebuquin betrat einen mühselig erleuchteten Raum, in dem eine Puppe stand, etwas dick, rot geschminkt mit gemalten Brauen, die seit ihrer Existenz eine Kusshand zuwarf. Erfreut über das Unkünstlerische setzte er sich auf einen Stuhl, einige Schritte von der Puppe entfernt. Der junge Mann wusste nicht, was ihn am Unkünstlerischen anzog. Er fand hier eine stille, freundliche Schmerzlosigkeit, die ihm jedoch gleichgültig war. Was ihn immer anzog, war der merkwürdige Umstand, dass ihn dies ruhig konventionelle Lächeln bewusstlos machen konnte. Ihn empörte die Ruhe alles Leblosen, da er noch nicht in dem nötigen Maasse abgestorben war, um für einen angenehmen Menschen gelten zu dürfen. Er schrie die Puppe an, beschimpfte sie und warf sie wieder einmal von ihrem Stuhl vor die Tür, wo die dicke Dame sie etwas besorgt aufhob. Er wand sich in der leeren Stube: »Ich will nicht eine Kopie, keine Beeinflussung, ich will mich, aus meiner Seele muss etwas ganz Eigenes kommen, und wenn es Löcher in eine private Luft sind. Ich kann nicht mit den Dingen etwas anfangen, ein Ding verpflichtet zu allen Dingen. Es steht im Strom, und furchtbar ist die Unendlichkeit eines Punktes.«

Die dicke Dame, Fräulein Euphemia, kam und bat ihn, fortzufahren, als ein dicker Herr ihn anfuhr:

»Jüngling, beschäftigen Sie sich mit angewandten Wissenschaften.«

Peinlich ging ihm das Talglicht eines Verstehens auf, dass er, wo er ein Schauspiel sehen wollte, einem anderen zum Theater gedient habe. Er schrie auf:

»Ich bin ein Spiegel, eine unbewegte, von Gaslaternen glitzernde Pfütze, die spiegelt. Aber hat ein Spiegel sich je gespiegelt?«

Mitleidig blickte ihn der Korpulente an. Er hatte einen kleinen Kopf, eine silberne Hirnschale mit wundervoll ziselierten Ornamenten, in welche feine, glitzernde Edelstein-

platten eingelassen waren. Giorgio wollte entweichen; Nebukadnezar Böhm schrie ihn wutvoll an:

»Was springen Sie so in meiner Atmosphäre herum,
Unmensch?«

»Verzeihung, mein Herr, Ihre Atmosphäre ist ein Produkt
von Faktoren, die in keiner Beziehung zu Ihnen stehen.«

»Wenn auch«, erwiderte liebenswürdig Nebukadnezar,
»es ist eine Machtfrage, eine Sache der Benennung, der
Selbsthypnose.«

Bebuquin richtete sich auf.

»Sie sind wohl aus Sachsen und haben Nietzsche gelesen,
der darüber, dass man ihm das Polizeiressort nicht anvertraute,
wahnsinnig wurde und in die Notlage kam, psychologisch
scharfsinnige Bücher zu schreiben.«

Fräulein Euphemia bat die Herren, mit ihrem Geist rationeller
umzugehen, und sie wolle gern ein Ball-Lokal besuchen. Die
beiden nickten und stampften die Holztreppe hinunter.

Euphemia holte einen Abendmantel, und Nebukadnezar
ergriff ein Sprachrohr und bellte in die sich breit aufrollende
Milchstrasse:

»Ich suche das Wunder.« Der Schosshund Euphemias fiel aus
dem Sprachrohr; Euphemia kehrte angenehm lächelnd zurück.

»Beste«, meinte Nebukadnezar, »Erotik ist die Ekstase des
Dilettanten; ich werde Sie aber in meinem nächsten Feuilleton
protegieren. Die Frauen sind immer aufreibend, da sie stets
dasselbe geben, und wir nie glauben wollen, dass zwei ganz
verschiedene Körper das gleiche Zentrum besitzen.«

»Adieu, ich will Sie nicht hindern, Ihre Betrachtungen
durch die Tat zu beweisen.«

Euphemia bat, dass der Dicke etwas zu trinken und zu
essen aus dem Hotel hole, und kehrte um, ihren Hund zu

pflegen, von dessen Unfall sie hörte. Der Dicke ergriff einen Baum und schmerzlich an den Hals. Dann ging auch er, den Hund pflegen. –

Nebukadnezar neigte den Kopf über Euphemias massigen Busen. Ein Spiegel hing über ihm. Er sah, wie die Brüste sich in den feingeschliffenen Edelsteinplatten seines Kopfes zu mannigfachen fremden Formen teilten und blitzten, in Formen, wie sie ihm keine Wirklichkeit bisher zu geben vermochte. Das ziselierte Silber brach und verfeinerte das Glitzern der Gestalten. Nebukadnezar starrte in den Spiegel, sich gierig freuend, wie er die Wirklichkeit gliedern konnte, wie seine Seele das Silber und die Steine waren, sein Auge der Spiegel. »Bebuquin«, schrie er und brach zusammen; denn er vermochte immer noch nicht, die Seele der Dinge zu ertragen. Zwei Arme zerrten ihn auf, pressten ihn an zwei feste breite Brüste, und lange Haarsträhnen fielen über seinen Silberschädel, und jedes Haar waren tausend Formen. Er erinnerte sich der Frau und merkte etwas beklemmt, dass er nicht mehr zu ihr dringen könne durch das Blitzen der Edelsteine, und sein Leib barst fast im Kampfe zwei Wirklichkeiten. Dabei überkam ihn eine wilde Freude, dass ihm sein Gehirn aus Silber fast Unsterblichkeit verlieh, da es jede Erscheinung potenzierte, und er sein Denken ausschalten konnte, dank dem präzisen Schliff der Steine und der vollkommen logischen Ziselierung. Mit den Formen der Ziselierung konnte er sich eine neue Logik schaffen, deren sichtbare Symbole die Ritzen der Kapsel waren. Es vervielfachte seine Kraft, er glaubte in einer anderen, immer neuen Welt zu sein mit neuen Lüsten. Er begriff seine Gestalt im Tasten nicht mehr, die er fast vergessen, die sich in Schmerzen wand, da die gesehene Welt nicht mit ihr übereinstimmte.

»Missbrauchen Sie mich, bitte, nicht«, klang die dünne Stimme Bebuquins im Spiegel, »regen Sie sich nicht so an Gegenständen auf; es ist ja nur Kombination, nichts Neues. Wüten Sie nicht mit deplazierten Mitteln; wo sind Sie denn? Wir können uns nicht neben unsere Haut setzen. Die ganze Sache vollzieht sich streng kausal. Ja, wenn uns die Logik losliesse; an welcher Stelle mag die einsetzen; das wissen wir beide nicht. Da steckt das Beste. Beinahe wurden Sie originell, da Sie beinahe wahnsinnig wurden. Singen wir das Lied von der gemeinsamen Einsamkeit. Ihre Sucht nach Originalität entspringt Ihrer beschämenden Leere; meine auch. Ich entziehe mich Ihnen ohne weiteres. Dann spiegeln Sie sich in sich selbst. Sie sehen, das ist ein Punkt. Aber die Dinge bringen uns auch nicht weiter.«

Spitzengardinen werden zusammengezogen.

ZWEITES KAPITEL

Bebuquin wälzte sich in den Kissen und litt.

Er machte sich daran, zunächst zu erfahren, was Leiden sei, wo für ihn das Leiden noch einen Grund und Zweck berge. Er fand aber keinen; denn so oft er den Schmerz zergliederte, traf er Ursachen, oder genauer, Umwandlungen an, die alles andere als Leiden waren. Er erkannte das Leiden als Stimulanz zur Freude, als angenehmes Ausgespannt-werden und sagte sich, dass nirgends ein Leiden aufzufinden wäre, und im Ganzen in einer solchen Bezeichnungsweise eine lächerliche Naivität des Vermischens liege; dass das Logische nichts mit dem Seelischen zu tun habe, fiel ihm auf; dass es eine gefälschte Zurechtmachung wäre. Er fand das Logische so schlecht wie Maler, die für die Tugend ein blondes Frauenzimmer hinsetzen.

»Der Fehler des Logischen ist, dass es noch nicht einmal symbolisch gelten kann. Man muss einsehen, ihr Dummköpfe, dass die Logik nur Stil werden darf, ohne je eine Wirklichkeit zu berühren. Wir müssen logisch komponieren, aus den logischen Figuren heraus wie Ornamentkünstler. Wir müssen einsehen, dass das Phantastischste die Logik ist.«

Ein Grauen überlief ihn, da er der Gegenstände gedachte, die ihn stets aufsaugen wollen; wie er die Gegenstände durch seine Symbolik vernichte, und wie alles nur in der Vernichtung existiere. Hier sah er eine Berechtigung alles Aesthetischen; aber zugleich auch, dass er, da er keinen ganzen Endzweck mehr sah, den einzelnen leugnen musste. Er sehnte sich nach dem Wahnsinn, doch seinen letzten ungezügelten Rest Mensch ängstigte es sehr. Seine einzige Rettung schien eine anständige Langeweile zu sein; aber nicht, um sich damit wie der lebensfrohe Schopenhauer die Berechtigung zu einem System zu erschleichen; obwohl ihm klar wurde, dass in der Langeweile ein Stilfaktor ersten Ranges latent sei. Er blätterte in einigen Mathematikbüchern, und viele Freude bereitete es ihm, mit der Unendlichkeit umherzuspringen, wie Kinder mit Bällen und Reifen. Hier glaubte er in keinem Hinübergehen in die Dinge zu stehen, er merkte, dass er in sich sei.

Er sah ein, dass es verfehlt sei, sich Dichter zu nennen; dass er in der Kunst immer im Rausch der Symbole bleibe. Es genügte ihm keineswegs, dass die Technik der Poesie symbolisch sei, und ihre Gegenstände damit einen ganz anderen Sinn erhielten; noch immer fand er, dass die sprachliche Darstellung eben nur unreine Kunst sei, gemessen an der Musik. Er verwünschte die Anstrengungen der Wissenschaftler, die Musik auf reale physiologische Vorgänge zurückzuführen. Aber es berührte ihn entschieden angenehm, dass sie ihre Verdauung interpretierten, doch alles Künstlerische mit grosser Sicherheit umgingen. Es freute ihn, wie sich hier eine alte Meinung bestätigte, dass die Teile über das Ganze gar nichts aussagten, das Synthetische in der logischen Analyse die unbewusste Voraussetzung sei, und man gerade die Hauptsache somit sicher umgehe, wie es diese Psychologen taten.

Traurig rief er aus, »welch schlechter Romanstoff bin ich, da ich nie etwas tun werde, mich in mir drehe; ich möchte gern über Handeln etwas Geistreiches sagen, wenn ich nur wüsste, was es ist. Sicher ist mir, dass ich noch nie gehandelt oder erlebt habe.«

»Auch nie genossen, Idiot«, fauchte Nebukadnezar in die Stube, und schlug wieder den Deckel des Nachtstuhles zu. Leuchtende kleine Wolken glühten auf, und ein Vorhang aus Mull mit zarten Blumen überdeckt, wurde auseinandergezogen.

»Mein Herr, Sie faselten eben von einer reinlichen Scheidung Ihres Ichs. Ich merke, Sie suchen Gott. Nun ja, ich gestehe, es ist schwer einzusehen, dass alles Relative eben durch den Genuss und ähnliche passive Räusche absolut wird. Den Weg zu Dingen zu vergessen, haben Sie eben noch nicht fertig gebracht, aber die Resultate sind gleich, Sie Säugling mit der Denkerstirn«, schrie er mit erhobenem Zeigefinger. »Ich habe mich noch nie dafür interessiert, was ich geniesse, aber dass ich geniesse, war mir stets von grösster Wichtigkeit.«

»Mein Herr, Sie suchen Zwecke mit Ihrem Bauch. Entfernen Sie sich. Im übrigen war Ihre jenseitige Genussmaschine gefährlich. Ich wohnte doch Ihrem seligen Abscheiden bei.«

»Sie sehen also immer noch nicht ein, dass lediglich die Nervenstränge rissen. Mein zieseliertes Hirn war bei weitem dauerhafter. Es ist empörend, dass Ihr misslicher Ernst mich stets zu faulen Witzen reizt. Jetzt haben Sie Ihre eigenste Spiegelung weg.«

Er setzte sich zu Bebuquin ins Bett.

»Bebuquin«, begann er gütig, »Sie sind ja immer noch ein Mensch. Variieren Sie doch einmal, monotoner Kloss. Gestatten Sie mir, dass ich Ihnen von den Gärten der Zeichen, die Geschichte von den Vorhängen erzähle. Narzissus, Unproduktiver.«

Giorgo zog sich die Decke von den Ohren, steckte einen Kakes in den Mund, und Böhm hub an:

DRITTES KAPITEL
DIE GESCHICHTE VON DEN VORHÄNGEN

Ich stand vor einem grossen Stück aus Sackleinwand und schrie: »Knoten seid ihr.«

»Müssen Sie denn immer schimpfen?«

»Unterbrechen Sie mich nicht. Aber ich habe das Bedürfnis, mich zu dokumentieren. Bald merkte ich es, dass niemand anders die Sackleinwand sei, als ich. Es war die erste Selbsterkenntnis. Aber ich drang weiter. Ein grosses Gepolter begann. Ein Sturm zerriss mich. Ich schrie vor Schmerz. Ich merkte, wie der grösste Teil der Leinwand zum Teufel ging. Aber dann war ich total von mir geblendet. Denken Sie, ich war ein stählernes Gebirge, das auf dem Kopf stand. Zarte Seelenblumen cachierten die Abgründe, die mit keinem Schock Sofakissen auszufüllen waren. Ich begriff den ganzen Unsinn und merkte, dass ein Sandkorn bei weitem wertvoller sei, als eine unendliche Welt. Es ging mir auch das Infinitesimale, das Wunder der Qualität, auf, das weder historisch, noch sonst wie aufgelöst werden kann. Jedenfalls merkte ich mir, dass es lediglich auf eine möglichst ungehinderte Bewegung ankomme. Ich gestehe zu, dass hier das Logische nicht ausreicht, weil jedes Axiom das andere widerlegt. Denken Sie daran, dass man mit dem Satze vom kausalen Denken eben gerade auf das Unkausale kommt, aber mit grüner Ergebung gehe ich auf die Hauptsache los. Ich sagte mir, Böhm werde dich los. Alles Persönliche ist unproduktiv. Sei Vorhang und zerreisse dich. Beschimpfe dich so lange, bis du etwas anderes bist. Sei Vorhang und Theaterstück zugleich. Wenn du eine Sehnsucht hast, dann handle stets im umgekehrten Sinn; denn sonst steckst du zu bald im Leim. Ich habe es stets gesagt, das Umgekehrte ist genau so richtig. Aber gehen Sie nicht mehr auf zwei Beinen. Warum amputieren Sie nicht eins heroisch unter der Bettdecke weg? Genuss verlangt Selbstbeherrschung und Qual.

Grundsatz: vermeiden Sie das Gleichgewicht.

Sie sehen, meine silberne Gehirnschale ist asymmetrisch. Darin liegt meine Produktivität. Über den sich fortwährend verändernden Kombinationen verlieren Sie das unglückselige Gedächtnis für die Dinge und den peinlichen Hang zum Endgültigen. Was Sie bisher nicht zu denken wagten. Die Welt ist das Mittel zum Denken. Es handelt sich nicht um Erkennen, das ist eine phantastische Tautologie. Hier geht es um Denken, Denken. Dadurch ändert sich die ganze Affäre, mein Herr. Genies handeln nie, oder sie handeln nur scheinbar. Ihr Zweck ist ein Gedanke, ein neuer, neuester Gedanke.

Mein Herr, verstehen Sie jetzt den grossen Napoleon? Der Mann war nicht ehrgeizig. Das ist die Projektion der Universitätsintriguen und der Dilettanten. Der Mann versuchte immer neue Mittel, um denken zu können; aber er war etwas Ideologe. Nur eines bitte ich mir aus: werfen Sie mich nicht mit der haltlosen Gefühlsduselei eines Pantheisten zusammen. Diese Leute haben nie ein gutes Bild begriffen; da steckt ihr Fehler. Das sind unkonzentrierte Gymnasiasten, die deswegen über einen Begriff nicht hinauskommen, und gerade den leugne ich. Der Begriff ist gerade so ein Nonsens, wie die Sache. Man wird nie die Kombinaton los. Der Begriff will zu den Dingen, aber gerade das Umgekehrte will ich. Ich richte meine Aufmerksamkeit auf den Genuss. Sie wissen nun, dass mein Ende fast als ein tragisches zu bezeichnen ist. Ziehen Sie sich aber an. Wir wollen einer hypothetischen Handlung beiwohnen, nämlich meinem Seelenamt.«

VIERTES KAPITEL

Seit Wochen starrte Bebuquin in einen Winkel seiner Stube, und er wollte den Winkel seiner Stube aus sich heraus beleben. Es graute ihn, auf die unverständlichen, niemals endenden Tatsachen angewiesen zu sein, die ihn verneinten Aber sein erschöpfter Wille konnte nicht ein Stäubchen erzeugen; er konnte mit geschlossenen Augen nichts sehen.

»Es muss möglich sein, genau wie man früher an einen Gott glauben konnte, der die Welt aus nichts erschuf. Wie peinlich, dass ich nie vollkommen sein kann. Doch warum fehlt mir sogar die Illusion der Vollkommenheit.« Da merkte er, dass eine gewisse Vorstellungsfähigkeit des Tatsächlichen noch in ihm sei. Er bedauerte dies, wiewohl ihm alles gleichgültig erschien. Es war nicht, dass die generellen Instinkte in ihm abgestorben wären. Er sagte sich, dass der Wert etwas Alogisches sei, und er wollte damit nicht Logik machen. Er spürte in diesem Widerspruch keine Belebung, sondern Aufhebung, Ruhe. Nicht die Verneinung machte ihm Vergnügen. Er verachtete diese prätentiösen Nörgler. Er verachtete diese Unreinlichkeit des dramatischen Menschen. Er sagte sich, vielleicht nötige ihn nur seine Faulheit zu dieser Betrachtung. Doch die Gründe waren ihm nebensächlich. Es handelte sich um den Gedanken, der logisch war, woher auch seine Ursachen kamen.

Böhm begrüsste ihn leise und freundlich. Er wollte sich nach seinem Tode etwas schonen, da er noch nichts Sicheres über die Unsterblichkeit wusste. »Es ist anständig und lässt Sie in gutem Licht erscheinen, wie Sie sich mit Todesverachtung um das Logische bemühen. Aber leider dürften Sie keinen Erfolg haben, da Sie nur eine Logik und ein Nichtlogisches annehmen. Es gibt viele Logiken, mein Lieber, in uns, welche sich bekämpfen, und aus deren Kampf das Alogische hervorgeht. Lassen Sie sich nicht von einigen mangelhaften Philosophen täuschen, die fortwährend von der Einheit schwatzen und den Beziehungen aller Teile aufeinander, ihrem Verknüpftsein zu einem Ganzen. Wir sind nicht mehr so phantasielos, das Dasein eines Gottes zu behaupten. Alles unverschämte Einbiegen auf eine Einheit appelliert nur an die Faulheit der Mitmenschen. Bebuquin, sehen Sie einmal: Vor allen Dingen wissen die Leute nichts von der Beschaffenheit des Leibes. Erinnern Sie sich der weiten Strahlenmäntel der Heiligen auf den alten Bildern und nehmen Sie diese bitte wörtlich. Doch das alles sind Gemeinplätze. Was Ihnen, mein

Lieber, fehlt, ist das Wunder. Merken Sie jetzt, warum Sie von allen Sachen und Dingen abgleiten? Sie sind ein Phantast mit unzureichenden Mitteln. Auch ich suchte das Wunder. Denken Sie an Melitta, die aus dem Sprachrohr fiel, und wie ich mich blamierte. Man braucht die Frauen überhaupt nur, um sich zu blamieren. Es ist das eine Selektion, die gerecht ist, gerade weil in der Frau nur Dummheit steckt. Darum redet man bei ihr von Möglichkeiten und meint zuletzt, dass die Frau phantastisch sei. Hinter eines kam ich seit meinem seligen Abscheiden. Sie sind Phantast, weil Sie nicht genug können. Das Phantastische ist gewiss ebenso Stoff- wie Formfrage. Aber vergessen Sie eines nicht. Phantasten sind Leute, die nicht mit einem Dreieck zu Ende kommen. Man soll nicht sagen, dass sie Symbolisten sind. Aber in Gottes Namen, Ihnen ist dieser Dilettantismus nötig. Sie sahen noch nie ein paar Leute, nie ein Blatt. Denken Sie eine Frau unter der Laterne; eine Nase, ein Lichtbauch, sonst nichts. Das Licht, aufgefangen von Häusern und Menschen. Damit wäre noch etwas zu sagen. Hüten Sie sich vor quantitativen Experimenten. In der Kunst ist die Zahl, die Grösse ganz gleichgültig. Wenn sie eine Rolle spielt, so ist sie bestimmt abgeleitet. Mit der Unendlichkeit zu arbeiten, ist purer Dilettantismus. Hier gebe ich Ihnen noch einen Ratschlag, der Sie später vielleicht anregt. Kant wird gewiss eine grosse Rolle spielen. Merken Sie sich eins. Seine verführerische Bedeutung liegt darin, dass er Gleichgewicht zustande brachte zwischen Objekt und Subjekt. Aber eines, die Hauptsache vergass er: was wohl das Erkenntnistheorie treibende Subjekt macht, das eben Objekt und Subjekt konstatiert. Ist das wohl ein psychisches Ding an sich. Da steckt der Haken, warum der deutsche Idealismus Kant dermassen übertreiben konnte. Unschöpferische werden sich stets an Unmöglichen erschöpfen. Keine Grenzen kennen, wieviel Seelisches die Gegenstände ertragen, verantworten können. Alle Unendlichkeitsrederei kommt von ungeformter arbeitsloser Seelenenergie. Es ist der Ausdruck der potentiellen Energie, also eine Sache des kräftigen Nichtkönnens.«

FÜNFTES KAPITEL

Um die Tische verbanden sich die Wiener Rohrstühle zu rhythmischen Guirlanden. Die Nase eines Trinkers konzentrierte die Kette jäh. Die Lichter hingen klumpenweise von der Decke und zerplatzten die Wände zu Fetzen. »So vernichtet eins den anderen«, bemerkte hierzu der jugendliche Maler Heinrich Lippenknabe.

»Ich bin darauf dressiert, überall die Negation aufzufinden.

Ja, trotzdem: die Gemütlichkeit der Vernichtung ist das Interessanteste. Lachhaft ist die Gespanntheit von allem. Ich bedaure, dass sich Kunst und Philosophie die Aufgabe stellen, dies immer Fragmentarische als ruhende Form zu geben. In unserem Energieverbrauch muss es Teilungsgewohnheiten geben. Die Energie der Form verbirgt oft allzu heftige Angst vor Erweiterung, beweist den Rhythmus der Müdigkeit.

Immer beschäftigte es mich, alles nur vorläufig zu betrachten. Immer stiess ich auf Zustände der Völker, wo diese ablassend von strengen Werten nach kurzer Irre sich der Kunst zuwandten und hier sich Absolutes erschlichen mit dem Unterbewusstsein, dies sei erlaubt; sie führten nämlich ihre aesthetischen Gründe an in artistischem Sinne. Bald vergassen sie diese und hatten gemächliche Werte, auf denen es sich bequem ausruhen, arbeiten und leben liess. Das Aesthetische reagierte ethisch ab, zunächst mit Übertreibungen.

Ich gestehe, mit Vergnügen bemerkte ich, dass sich aus der symbolischen Kunst eine Formkunst bei einigen Begabteren abtrennte; aber vielleicht schuf das Symbol das Artistische, da dieses die Grenzenlosigkeit des ersteren überwinden musste, woraus sich die heutige Scheidung ergibt.

Fiel es Ihnen nicht auf, dass die früheren Christen durch die Bilder disputieren und denken; und gerade darum waren sie zur grössten Energie der Form und zur beständigen sinnlichen Variation eines in sich stille Bleibenden gezwungen.«

Bebuquin sagte: »Das Verdienst Schopenhauers, die Ruhe als Wesen aller Dinge und Subjekte eingeführt zu haben, ist stets hervorzuheben. Er gab damit die unbewegte Idee Platos wieder, das strenge, unberührte Gesetz; aber fürwahr, das Wesen ist ein Nichts. Doch ist die Reduzierung auf Eindrücke peinlich. Schwerlich werde ich mir einmal über den Produktiven klar. Dieses kindliche Suchen nach einem Anfang wird mich schädigen.«

Euphemia trat in das Café ein. Das gelbe Licht gab ihren Röcken, – die sich wie Wogen von Rudern bewegten, über ihren straffen Beinen schäumten, – Konturen, die in ihrem Hut zusammenliefen und an dem weit überhängenden Feder- bouquet ihres Hutes versprühten. Man hatte sie seit langem nicht mehr gesehen, da sie mit einem Knaben niedergekommen war. Die Geburt war für ihren Körper anscheinend vorteilhaft gewesen. Unwillkürlich dachte Bebuquin, an dem Kinde habe sie sich ihres Fettes, ihrer bisherigen schlechten Erfahrungen entledigt. Sie sah geradezu jungfräulich aus.

»Was ist doch das für ein Unglück, dass wir Männer vom Weibe kommen.«

Euphemia: »Nun, mein Junge, wie habe ich mich erholt?«

Heinrich Lippenknabe hub aber ein Lied an, das der bleiche lange Piccolo mit dem Rauschen der Vorhänge und dem Klingen der metallenen Schnürgriffe akzentuierte.

»Weit stinkt uns die Einsamkeit entgegen.

Auf allen unseren grauen Wegen

Krallt unser Auge sich an einen blauen Fleck,

die Einsamkeit,

Es ist ein dunkelklitschig Zimmer

ohne Wände, doch hat keiner ihre Höhe je ermessen.

Um uns tanzt der Kosmos voll Finessen,

Doch fällt auf mich kein Schimmer.«

»Hören Sie mit dem Blödsinn auf. Ich möchte die ganze Geschichte in mich konzentrieren.«

»Das können Sie ohne weiteres, glauben Sie es einfach.«

»Ich dachte schon oft, dass unsere Meinungen als strenge Umkehr der Tatsachen aufgefasst werden können.

Negation besagt gar nichts, ebensowenig die Bejahung. Das Künstlerische beginnt mit dem Worte anders. Künstlerische Formen können sich dermassen verfestigt haben, über die Dinge hinausgewachsen sein, dass sie einen neuen Gegenstand erschaffen. Ihnen ist die Welt zum Greuel geworden, die sich dem Maskenspiel des Dichters opfern soll. Aber wir sind in unser Gedächtnis eingeschlossen, auf Tautologien angewiesen – ich sehe dabei von der Existenz des Wortes »Form« ab.

Das Wesentliche dieses Wortes ist, dass es mit Nichts alles enthält, aber zugleich mehr ist als Begriff oder Symbol. Auf der einen Seite geht es über das Logische weit hinaus und lässt von der Erfahrung bedeutendere Merkmale zurück; sie besitzt Selbstbewegung. Ruhe und Bewegung sind zugleich in ihr eingeschlossen. Das Symbol gab die Vor- und Nachfolgen der

Form, das empirische und ein fremdes; die Form aber verbarg sich ungesehen zwischen den beiden Gliedern. Die Form weist auch über die Kausalität hinaus, zugleich besitzt sie vorzüglichere Eigenschaften, als die Idee; sie ist mehr als ein Prozess. Vor allem aber vermag sie sich mit jedem Organ und Ding zu verbinden; da ihre Verpflichtung an die Gegenstände eine denkbar lose ist, gebietet sie diesen ohne Vergewaltigung. In ihr beendet sich die christliche Verneinung der Gestalt; gerade jene wird von ihr erstrebt mit den reinen Kräften der Seele. Der Christ gab nie ein wenigstens scheinbares Endresultat, er verneinte und vergewaltigte krampfhaft. Vielleicht gebiert die Form neue Gegenstände; sie ist von ihrem Ursprünglichen entfernter, als der Begriff, und eine Deduktion von ihr ist durchaus von einer begrifflichen unterschieden. Die Anschauung gewinnt in ihr eine Kraft, die vorher dem Begriff allein zugesprochen wurde.«

SECHSTES KAPITEL

Eine blaue Hutfeder Euphemias besoff sich blitzend in der grünen Chartreuse.

Bebuquin schaute mit seinem linken Bein in die Ecke der Bar, wo Heinrich Lippenknabe nachdenkerisch in die bronzierte Nabelhöhle einer Hetäre eine Orchidee arrangierte und sie mit Kognak begoss.

»Wer ist der Vater?« schrie die Buffetdame.

Der Schein der elektrischen Lampen fuhr ihr durch die Spitzen zum Knie, tanzte über die Kristallflacons und die Sektkühler erregt rückwärts; das sonst anständige elektrische Licht!

»Keiner«, schaute Euphemia mit kreisförmig ausgebreiteten Augen. »Ich kriegte ihn im Traum.«

»Quatsch«, rief Heinrich Lippenknabe, »sie meint ein vergebliches Präventiv.«

»Erstens hatte ich keine Ahnung, wer der Vater sein kann. Das ist auch gleichgültig.« Sie sah erschreckt drein.

»War es vielleicht Böhm?« fragte Bebuquin.

Euphemia schrie senkrecht auf.

»Der kommt immer, er wird das Kind stillen, er hat jetzt eine solch milchfarbene Schädelplatte, seit er starb, und er benutzt seinen Schlingdarm, für den er jetzt keine Verwendung mehr hat, als Zither und singt sehr ergreifend dazu den Pythagoreischen Lehrsatz. Er sagte, der Junge müsse ein ganz intellektueller werden.«

»Ja, dein Embryo schrieb doch eine philosophische Arbeit und doktorierte auf Geburt; nicht wahr, die Geschichte heisst: die zerstörte Nabelschnur oder das principium individuationis.«

»Ja«, flüsterte Euphemia, »er hat bereits der Welt entsagt, er wird geistig, ist ganz wunschlos, unreinlich und schweigsam. Ausserdem hat er eine sensible Haut, die wechselt fortwährend Farbe. Kann man ihn nicht als Reklametransparent benutzen? Man spart farbige Glühlampen.«

»Das Alogische wächst, das Alogische siegt, er wird nicht abgeleitet.«

Bebuquin balanzierte auf dem kippligen Barstuhl.

»Darum, meine Damen, werden so viele verrückt. Wir entbehren der Fiktionen, der Positivismus ruiniert.«

Die Buffetdame kniete verzückt zwischen den Sektkühlern.

»Herr, wir konzipieren zu materiell.«

Ihr Spitzenkleid umglitzerte sie, Ornament des Traums.

Die Sektkühler, heilige Gefässe des Unsäglichen. »Wir opfern nichts mehr«, schrie Bebuquin auf die Strasse, »das Sublime geht verloren. Das Wunder kritisiert Ihr, das Wunder hat nur Sinn, wenn es leibhaftig ist, aber ihr habt alle Kräfte zerstört, die über das Menschliche hinausgehen.«

»Ich will, dass der Geist sichtbar werde«, stöhnte Heinrich Lippenknabe.

»Das Nichts soll sich materialisieren«, die Dame mit der Orchidee in der Nabelhöhle.

Böhm stand unter ihnen.

Er sagte:

»Das Naturgesetz soll sich im Alkohol besaufen, bis es merkt, es gibt irrationale Situationen, und einsieht, gesetzmässig ist nur der Demokrat mit dem Reichstagswahlrecht und die Schwachheit. Das Gesetz realisiert sich seelisch nie, es hängt sinnlos an dem Nagel irgend eines schlechten Mathematikaxioms.

Wenn etwas auf das Gesetz erkannt wird, beweist es nur, die Sache ist als Erlebnis überlebt. Das Gesetz ist die Vergangenheit, dem Tod unterworfen.

Sic.

Es fehlen uns die Ausnahmen.

Zu wenig Leute haben den Mut, vollkommenen Blödsinn zu sagen. Häufig wiederholter Blödsinn wird integrierendes Moment unseres Denkens; bei einer gewissen Stufe der Intelligenz interessiert man sich für das Korrekte, Vernünftige gar nicht mehr.

Die Vernunft macht zu viel Grosses, Erhabenes zum Grotesken, Unmöglichen. An der Vernunft ruinierten wir Gott die umfassende Idiosinkrasie.

Welches Recht hat die Vernunft dazu? Sie sitzt.

Auf der Einheit.

Da sitzt die Gemeinheit.

Es gibt so viele Welten, die gar nichts miteinander zu tun haben, so wenig, wie grüne Chartreuse mit den Visionen, in die sie sich umsetzt.

Wenn ein sympathischer Zeitgenosse sich mit Ausserordentlichem abgibt, sperren sie ihn ins Irrenhaus.

Meine Herren, der Mann interessiert sich nur nicht für Ihre rationale Welt. Warum wollen Sie denn nicht einsehen, wenigstens dass Ihre Vernunft langweilig ist?

Alles stilisiert die Vernunft, das meiste verschleisst sie zu angeblich belanglosen Übergängen, das andere ist Kanon, das Wertvolle, das Langweilige, Demokratische, das Stabile.

Meine Herren, die Intelligenz und Phantasie der Leute hat sich darin zu zeigen, dass man den Blitz einfängt, differenzieren Sie. Ich versichere Ihnen, ich zum Beispiel lebe nur, weil ich mich mir suggeriere; in Wirklichkeit bin ich tot. Sie wissen doch, ich liess mich einsargen. Aber ich versprach mir, als Reklame für das Unwirkliche herumzulaufen, bis irgend ein Idiot ein Wunder an mir erlebt. Sehet, Babys, unwirklich, nichts, das sind Bezeichnungen für eure schlechten Augen. Wenn es eine künftige Fülle gibt, dann kommt sie aus dem Nichts, dem Unwirklichen. Das ist die einzige Garantie für die Zukunft.

Der Utilist und der Vernünftler sagen für das Imaginäre Trug und Maja, für das Nichts Vacuum oder Aether. Das sind Leute, die wollen alles in den Mund nehmen und essen oder zu einer Moral aufschneiden. Aber das Nichts ist die indifferente Voraussetzung allen Seins. Das Nichts ist die Grundlage, nur darf man nicht an Robert Meyer glauben und alle Existenz ist doch nur eine Einschränkung des Nichts.

Die Existenz in Formen ist ein Sofa, eine Schlummerrolle, eine ebenso unverbindliche, wie langweilende Konvention. Wenn man frei und kühn zum Leben in vielen Formen ist, wenn man den Tod als ein Vorurteil, einen Mangel an Phantasie ansieht, dann geht man aufs Phantastische, das ist die Unermüdlichkeit in allen möglichen Formen. Ich gebe zu, die Vernunft macht alles bequem, sie konzentriert, aber sie zerstört zu viel, macht zu vieles lächerlich und gerade das Grösste Man muss das Unmögliche so lange anschauen, bis es eine leichte Angelegenheit ist. Das Wunder ist eine Frage des Trainings.

Euphemia, euch mangelt ein Kult.

Der Romantiker sagt: seht, ich habe Phantasie, und ich habe Vernunft, ich bin sonderlich und sage mitunter Sachen, die es nicht gibt, wie euch das meine Vernunft hinten nach zeigt. Wenn ich sehr poetisch sein will, sage ich dann die Geschichte hat mir geträumt. Aber, das ist mein sublimstes Mittel, damit muss man sparen. Und dann kommen noch Masken und Spiegelbild als romantischer Apparat. Aber, Herrschaften, da ist Aethetizismus bei. Beim Romantiker macht man einen Schritt vorwärts und zwei zurück. Das ist ein zuckendes Klebpflaster. «

Er begoss die noch nicht Verschiedenen mit Absinth.

»Hier ein Mittel des Dilettanten. «

Bebuquin fuhr Euphemia an die Nase und umarmte sie zugleich leidenschaftlich.

Ein Sturmregen pointilliert die grossen Scheibenfenster.

»Wir bedürfen einer Sündflut.

Man hat bis jetzt die Vernunft benutzt, die Sinne zu vergröbern, die Wahrnehmung zu reduzieren, zu vereinfachen. Im ganzen, die Vernunft verarmte; die Vernunft verarmte

Gott bis zur Indifferenz; töten wir die Vernunft; die Vernunft hat den gestaltlosen Tod produziert, wo es nichts mehr zu sehen gibt. Noch für Dante war der Tod ein Vorwand für Glanz, Farbe, Reichtum und Lust. Nehmen wir unsere Sinne, entreissen wir sie der Ruhe der Stupidität platonischer Ideen, beobachten wir den Moment, der viel eigenartiger ist, als die Ruhe, weil er differenziert und charakteristisch ist, gar keine Einheit hat, sondern sich zwischen vorn und hinten restlos aufteilt.«

Der tote Böhm tanzte dankend auf Euphemias Hut und versank im Buffet; er legte sich wieder in eine seltsame Kognaksorte, die er von jeher geliebt.

SIEBENTES KAPITEL

Die drei Bogenlampen schweben in der Bar. Ihre Strahlen, losgelöst vom inneren Lichtkern, durchbohrten sich wie Stricknadeln. Böhm im Kognak stieg heraus, tanzte hinter den Kristallflacons der farbigen Schnäpse, leise trällernd den Cancan des Chamäleons serpentina alcoholica.

Die Monde der Bogenlampen wurden obscön, ihre Strahlen fingerten in der Dekolletage der Damen, man hörte auf Bebuquins leise trockene Stimme, der von seiner letzten Liebschaft erzählte.

»Der Abschied von der Symetrie.

Meine letzte Geliebte stand im Garten zur sympathischen Kurve – ist eine Vase aus Knidos. Ein reiches Weib besass sie, konnte sie aber nicht um sich ertragen, weil sie die Konkurrenz mit der Vase nicht bestreiten konnte. Sie stiess bedeutend mit der Zunge an und sah ästhetische Jünglinge bei sich. Um Bildung zu markieren, zeigte die Dame den Jünglingen stets die knidische Vase. Also die Jünglinge verglichen kunstgewerblich die Dame mit der Vase. Der Pot hatte unbedingt die Form eines schlanken Weibes, die Dame zog dabei den kürzeren und kam mit ihrer Liebe zur Kunst nicht auf ihre Kosten. Diese Vase ruinierte mich fast, meine Sinne waren ziemlich abstrakt gestimmt. Ich suchte wochenlang nach der Frau, welche die Proportionen der Vase habe. Selbstverständlich vergeblich. Höchstens die Puppe in Euphemias billiger Erstarrnis. Aber das stimmte alles nicht. Im Traum stieg ich zur Vase und zerbrach sie regelmässig. Das Gefäss machte mich zum Klassizisten, zum symmetrisch geteilten Stilisten. Da fand ich's. Die Symmetrie ist wie die platonische Idee eine tote Ruhe. Böhm sagte mal, ich sollte mir ein Bein amputieren. Das war brutal, aber ganz richtig. Doch die Sache war mir damals nicht klar, die Symmetrie ist langweilig wie Mechanik. Zuletzt liess ich mir die knidische Vase schenken. Damit war der Dame des Hauses und mir gedient. Nach einer ziemlich schlimmen Nacht schlug ich den Topf entzwei. Es ging ums Leben. Seitdem bin ich Romantiker geworden.«

Bebuquin sah gar nicht, dass die Hetäre und Euphemia krampfhaft unter den Bogenlampen sassen, Liköre tranken und in das Licht starrten. Lippenknabe küsste seine Maitresse auf den Arm. Grell schrie sie auf und wehrte den Maler deutlich mit einer langen, spitzen Hutnadel aus dem zuckenden Lichtkreis ab.

Er zog sich notgedrungen zurück.

Die Frauen lagen verzückt unter den starren, stechenden Dolchen der Bogenlampen.

Sie stöhnten wie Tiere.

Die Lampen begannen zu zucken, sie zischten.

Bebuquin drehte die Leitung ab.

Die Frauen schraken verstört auf.

Der Maler sagte eifersüchtig »Sonnenkult« und ging.

Bebuquin blieb mit den Frauen. Man trank weiter, der Alkohol redete wie Gott aus dem Munde der Propheten.

Der fahle Morgen betupfte die Scheiben.

Er krauchte die Häusermauern hinunter.

Die drei Leute ängstigten sich vor der Trennung.

Denn man geht erst, wenn die Erschöpfung vollendet ist.

Sie kauerten zusammen, eine kalte, feuchte Schlange zog sich immer enger um die drei.

Der Schrecken des Farbenwechsels der übergehenden Zeiten machte sie stumm. Die Nacht, welche die vom Licht übergrellten Gesichte liebt, starb in den Tag hinein. Man fühlte, man müsse die Nächte zu einem ernsten Training benutzen, denn die drei wollten um jeden Preis Visionäre werden, ganz unmenschlich sein. Sie waren ihres Körpers und seiner Formen unabweislich müde geworden und spürten, dass sie sich verzerren müssten.

Unter der blöden Sonne gingen die Grauen heim.

Die Landschaft war auf ein Brett gestrichen, die aufgerissenen Augen spürten nicht mehr vor Überreizung, dass es heller und klarer wurde. Das Licht der Glühlampen und die sie umhüllende Finsternis steckte noch in den Sehnerven. Bebuquin suchte weinend der Sonne in einen imaginären Bauch zu treten. Ein Brillant über Euphemias Décoleté fing das unverbrauchte Morgenlicht auf, konzentrierte das Licht. Giorgio erschrak vor der blitzenden, schrie »verflucht« und suchte ihre Wohnung auf. Die Hetäre zog allein weiter. Man liess sie unbenutzt stehen, sie spannte ihren pfaufarbenen

Schirm auf, sprang wild ein paarmal in die Höhe, dann fügte sie sich in die Fläche einer Litfass-Säule, sie war nur ein Plakat gewesen für die neueröffnete Animierkneipe »Essay«.

ACHTES KAPITEL

Durch die regengepeitschte Nacht fuhr in ihrem Auto die Schauspielerin Fredegonde Perlenblick. Sie hörte ausserdem auf den Namen Mah bei jüngeren Liebhabern, Lou, wenn sie dämonisch war, und Bea, wenn sie eine Familie zu ersetzen suchte. Sie fuhr mit zwei erschrecklich blendenden Scheinwerfern, die im glitschrigen Asphalt, in dessen Regenwasser die Schatten der letzten Trotteurs gaukelten, weisse Lichtgruben aufrissen. Ihre Autohuppe hatte entschieden dramatische Kraft. Der Chauffeur hielt einen tragischen Rezitationsstil inne, die Huppe hatte das dramatische R. Auf dem Dache des Kupees war ein Kintopp angebracht, der den verschlafenen Bürgern zeigte, wie die Schauspielerin Fredegonde Perlenblick sich auszog, badete und zu Bett ging. Ehe es dunkel wurde, erschien über dem Bett kalligraphisch »Endlich allein?« Unter der Bilderreihe des rasenden Kinema stand zum Beispiel »Ich trage den Strumpfhalter ›Ideal‹« oder sonst irgend eine wertvolle Empfehlung. Die Schauspielerin liess vor der Bar halten. Sie stieg aus, es war noch niemand da. Ihr erster zündender Blick, der das Lokal durchkreiste, blieb unerwidert.

Sie setzte sich hin und war schön für sich selbst.

Bebuquin stieg über die Schwelle.

»Gnädigste, Sie sitzen auf einer Hypothese.«

»Ja, ich bin wie ein verkleideter Knabe.«

Die Dame zog den Blick Nummer fünf. Sie merkte, diesmal müsste sie auf höherem Niveau einsetzen.

»Gnädigste, wissen Sie, Sie beweisen mir durchaus die Nichtexistenz des Materiellen.«

»Oh, wir werden ja auch beim Theater, soweit angängig, Stilisten. Ich habe schon ein Reformkleid versucht, aber das ist so schwer zu tragen. Entweder, man sieht wie permanente Jungfrau aus, oder schlechthin verheiratet. Ein Mittelstück gibt's da gar nicht.«

Sie markierte erregten Busen.

Man war still.

Der schalkige Böhm befunkelte aus seiner Kognakbütte den Hals Fredegondes. Sie reagierte. Bescheiden sprach er:

»Gnädigste, wollen Sie einen Edelstein aus meinem Kopf?«

»Ich habe den Büchmann und eine lyrische Anthologie. Das genügt«, sagte sie entrüstet.

»Ich meine ja ganz richtige.«

»Vorher musste ich auf einer Hypothese sitzen, und jetzt wollen Sie mir immaterielle Juwelen verzapfen. Mein Herr, achten Sie den Intellekt eines Weibes.«

»Kindchen, hast Du schon von einem verkehrten Kaffee gehört? Sieh, gönn uns den bescheidenen Sport der Verrücktheit.«

»Aber man muss natürlich sein. Ich bin immer so natürlich.« Jetzt lächelte sie bereits.

Böhm schnalzte ihr flink einen Edelstein auf den Hals und redete mit furchtbarer Stimme.

»Jetzt bist du in die Träume gezogen.

Schmerzkakadu los!«

Der Giebel des Buffets färbte sich bunt. Vogelaugen starrten, die Wände der Bar überzogen sich mit Vogelfedern, und man hörte ein Gerattel von Flügeln, man spürte, es wird geflogen, höher, wilder in dem Wahnsinn.

Die Schauspielerin schrie:

»Drehbühne! Shakespeare bei Reinhardt!« und hielt krampfhaft ihre Handtasche.

Die Flügel des Kakadus wurden mit Menschen angefüllt.

Euphemia sass über allen, Emil, den phosphoreszierenden Embryo, auf dem Schoss und rief:

»Herrschaften, heute wird schwarz weiss.

Wir werden so wütend, dass wir hintennach kein Wort mehr reden werden.

Oh, ich bin ja nur die Wachspuppe aus der billigen Erstarrnis.«

Jetzt sahen sie von sich ausgehend eine Reihe; es tanzten um sie die vergangenen Jahre, die rauften.

»Wir müssen auf die Sinne«, rief Böhm.

»Kinder, im Himmel gibt's nur verzückte Augen. Wir müssen so genau sehen, dass darin alles Wissen steckt.«

Aufgeregt starrte das Volk auf der Strasse nach dem grossen Tier, das in der Luft torkelte, und schrie:

»Es kommt der Lebendige.«

Der Vogel schrie in Graurot:

»Ich bin ein Beweis, es kann auch anders zugehen.«

Die Menschen klapperten vor Angst, ob sie es ertragen konnten.

Meistens bleibt man ja im dilettantischen Schrecken stecken.

Und endet mit einem Schlaganfall auf dem Plüschsofa.

Davor ein weisser Mops aus Porzellan.

Er hat eine rote Schleife.

NEUNTES KAPITEL

Aber selbstverständlich, man fliegt nicht immer. Beim vierten Glas rohen Wiskys sitzt man wieder schwer.

Euphemia sagte:

»Böhm ist doch ein törichter Mensch, ich weiss nie, ob er lebt oder tot ist.«

Drei Arbeiter klumpten in die Bar.

Das elektrische Licht erinnerte sie an das der Fabrik.

Sie hatten zu fordern. Einer langte sich eine Flasche Sekt.

Ein sensibler Kellner keifte. Er zuckte nervös mit dem Knie.

Sein Vater war Hausknecht in einem bürgerlichen Lokal.

»Meine Herren, Sie kennen nicht den Schmerzkakadu. Es ist nicht ratsam, sich zu betrinken.«

Eine rote Arbeiterbluse mit einem blaubeglühten Schädel dröhnte.

»Wir nippen bloss.«

Nahm einige Likörflaschen unter den Arm, und die Schauspielerin Fredigonde Perlenblick.

»Athlet«, stöhnte sie verzückt.

Euphemia sagte verächtlich apodiktisch:

»Kühe sind Wiederkäuer, sei es Heu, sei es Shakespeare. Kühe lieben Stiere.«

Man hörte von der Strasse die schimpfende Tragödie.

»Explosive Seele.«

Sie hob ihre Röcke sehr hoch.

Ihr Auto raste gierig davon.

Es rollte den Asphalt auf, glitschte über die Reflexe der Gaslampen und der letzten Bummler.

Jetzt mag d'Annunzio weiterschreiben.

In der Bar sang man den Cantus der Gottesstreiter, zur Erbauung und Stärkung von Böhms Leiche. Lippenknabe schmeckte die trabende Melodie auf der Zunge wie Ricinusöl.

»Böhm ruiniert uns jedes Formgefühl. Der Kerl ist doch tot, wenn er auch hier herumflunkert.«

Man brach eine begonnene Debatte ab. Herein kam eine Dame, hintendrein ein dünner, ziemlich durchsichtiger Herr.

Er stellte sich mit dem Gesicht in eine Ecke und litaneite.

»Ehmke Laurenz, Platoniker gehe nur Nachts aus, weil es da keine Farben gibt. Ich suche die reine ruhende einsame Idee, diese Dame tatkräftig rhythmische Erregung. Ich bin eigentümlich, da ich von zwei Dingen ruiniert werde, einem höheren der Idee und einem niederen der Dame.«

»Ja, aber ruinieren Sie doch die beiden, die sich bedingen, zum mindesten Ihre blödsinnige Ideologie vom Sein, von der Langeweile, dem Tod. Das ist nur eine Müdigkeit, ein Defekt, Platonismus ist Anaesthesie. Reissen Sie sich doch die Augen aus und die Ohren, dann haben Sie Ihren Platonismus zu Wege gebracht.«

Aurora, die Frau des Kauzes, der prinzipiell farblose Schnäpse trank, näherte sich und sagte:

»Ehmke macht kontemplativ.« Ehmke schrak zusammen, blickte sie erst flehend, dann voll Verachtung an, sagte: »Du kennst mich nicht« – aber sie »dafür Du mich«; er grinste wie ein kleiner Idiot, senkte den Kopf zum Nabel, die Farbe ging ihm aus dem Gesicht, und schaute gelassen auf seinen Bauch.

Inzwischen war sie liebevoll.

Da die beiden schliesslich störten, liess man sie hinauswerfen, denn nichts ist so überflüssig, langweilig, wie ein Ideologe und eine Hure. Beide haben die banalste Form des Spleens.

Nach kurzer Weile kam ein Fremder ins Lokal, unauffällig im Frack wie jeder.

Böhm tänzelte bald aus der Cognaksorte und rief: »Das ist er.«

Euphemia ging wie in der Hypnose auf den Unbekannten zu und sagte: »Sie sind uns ganz fremd, aber furchtbar deutlich, ich soll mich Ihnen geben.«

Der Fremde sagte mit mittlerer Stimme:

»Bitte kommen Sie mit mir.«

»Und warum sollen wir Gott nicht lieben«, sagte leise Bebuquin.

»Denn das Unbekannte ist der Liebling des forschenden Schöpfers«, flüsterte Lippenknabe.

Die Uhr tönte die Sekunden, jede Sekunde war plastisch deutlich, das Auge sah den Klang. Die Erde war ihnen einen Augenblick ein kristallen Feuer, die Menschen von durchsichtigem Glas.

Bebuquin seufzte. Gegen die Scheiben fiel aus dem farbigen Morgenwind der beginnende Regen.

ZEHNTES KAPITEL

Die Menschen, die löffelweise, keiner wusste vom anderen, in den Zirkus, eine kolossalische Rotunde des Staunens, geflattert waren, sassen zur Masse verkeilt, und man erwartete Miss Euphemia. An den Ranggeländern liefen Ornamente erregter Hände entlang, Bogenlampen schwangen ihre energetischen Milchkübel.

Man bemerkte Miss Euphemia erst, als sie an die Decke aufgezogen war, sie hielt sich mit den Zähnen in einen Strick verbissen.

Liess sich los, und ein Salto mortale war an der Decke geschlagen zum anderen Ende, wo sie mit den Zähnen ein Seil aufriss.

Es fiel ein Programm.

Miss Euphemia glitt beim dritten Male am Seil ab; sie beschloss aus formalen Gründen, sich das Genick zu brechen.

Senkrecht schrien die Leute, einige versuchten, von den Galerien herabzuspringen. Euphemia sah den schwebenden Kronleuchter und ergriff fünfeinhalb Meter über dem Boden das Seil.

Die Leute wüteten.

Euphemia machte dann mit grosser Sicherheit noch einige Salto mortales.

Trotzdem, sie war moralisch ruiniert.

(Die stärkste Moralität dies des Handwerks).

Und sie fand es ziemlich, in ein Kloster einzutreten, um zu büssen.

Die Menschen leerten sich in dem kühlen Abend, gingen auseinander und verschwanden.

Der Zirkus stand leer, eine runde Dunkelheit.

Vor einem schlafenden Affenkäfig geisselte sich Euphemia.

ELFTES KAPITEL

Der Schatten eines sich begattenden Affenpaares schlich von der anderen Seite über Euphemia. Sie erschauerte müde, aber mit schattender Begierde, die über sie weg kroch. Leise ging sie in die Mitte der Arena, zog ihr Gazekleid ab und stand nackt in der Dunkelheit. Wenige spärliche Sterne leuchteten durch die Luken. Das verhängnisvolle Seil pendelte zwischen ihnen.

»Sie sind nun erledigt«, rief Bebuquin durch die Finsternis. Sein Schatten glitt über den Boden, über Euphemia.

»Rühren Sie mich nicht an«, schrie sie. »Ich gehöre dem andern. Ich habe mich dem imaginierten Böhm angetraut. Er kann aus der Wand kommen. Er ist ausserhalb jeder Regel. Er hat mir alles verwirrt. Sein tödlicher formloser Humor, bei dem jedes nichts und sehr bedeutungsvoll ist, fuhr in mich. Ich leide so unter den Versuchungen der Phantasie. Ein Weib hält das doch nicht aus. Sehen Sie, Böhm ist für mich wirklicher, wie Sie. Er ist ein grausamer Witz, eine phantastische Guillotine. O du mein Galgen. Ich sehe immer gerade aus, wie er's braucht. Er nimmt mir alle Kraft aus den Gliedern. Ich hocke tagelang und sehe ihn in dem Schatten des Abends, bald grünt er im Morgen, wie ein endloser Kakadu, bald liegt er draussen im Meer, und ich reise tagelang der Welle nach, der grünen Flasche, die ihn umschliesst. Es ist so reich, mit den Toten zu verkehren, es ist eine stille, innerlich bohrende Lust, lautlos sprengende Raserei; Böhm!«

»Ihnen sind die Gestalten verwirrt.«

»O Sie sind töricht, ich stehe in einem langen alten Mythus, der mich umschlingt wie ein Gewebe. Wissen Sie, die Luft ist etwas ganz anderes, das ist eine Glasglocke. Ich muss dahinaus, man erstickt so elend in dem engen Leben. Böhm erweiterte in einem ständigen Training die phantastischen Fähigkeiten seines Körpers; seine Stimme, die Strahlen seiner Augen. Ja, was war das, wie weit reichten die; ich bin einfach verfallen in die Grenzenlosigkeit des Humors. Doch ich leide unter all dem Grauenhaften. Ich vermöchte mit einem zufriedenen Lächeln irgendeinen zu töten, vielleicht nähme das alle Last von mir. Wissen Sie, wir handeln immer doch zuletzt aus einem Minimum von Überspannung, die eines findet, an dem sie sich auslöst. Eine grosse Dunkelheit und ein weniges, ein Grammchen von Überspannung. In uns sind alle Laster, alle Grösse, nur temperiert, gegenseitig geschwächt; aber wenn sich eins überspannt, der Hass, die Angst, die Liebe, dann ist es in einem Blitz den ganzen Weg durchgeflogen, oder wir gehen wie Mondsüchtige, haben die anderen Empfindungen verlernt, tun das Nötige und sind wie vorher und wissen nichts. So geschehen viele Morde.«

»Aber der Körper, die Sinne.«

»Du, mein Gott, das sind die ärmlichsten Gewöhnungen, Vorurteile. Viel stärker, reizvoller, gefährlicher sind die Empfindungen, die keines Erlebnisses bedürfen. Denn schliesslich gibt es Menschen, die kommen auf die Erde und kennen alles. Das Leben ist nur eine mühevoolle Darstellung der Erinnerung, nichts Neues.«

»Also kämen wir doch von Gott.«

»Aber woher denn?«

»Sie kriegten doch Emil.«

»Nein, das war nicht ich, irgend etwas in mir produzierte da, bewahrte auf. Und der erste Schrei des Kindes, das konnte doch nicht von mir kommen. Und die Form, der Körper, das ist doch nur ein Mittel, eine Ausdrucksform und ein schlechtes Instrument. Wenn ich mit Gott und Böhm mehr zusammen bin, werde ich das Meiste viel genauer kennen.«

»So geht alles von den Lebendigen weg zu den Toten. Die stehen eben energisch voran. Weisst Du, Euphemia, wie Du die Dessous oft behaglich abstreiftest. So fällt alles mögliche von mir ab. Man steht einfach gerade da, den Kopf über den Wolken und ist mehr oder weniger fertig. Es geht von einem weg. Die Leute, Wünsche, Quälereien, und man ist wie eine geleerte Pappschachtel. So weist Du, die Dunkelheit und die

Sonne, das sind für mich keine Gegensätze mehr, sind ein totes Gefühl, bald in Schwarz, bald in Weiss. Ich möchte mal schreien, dass die Tiger vor Angst ausbrechen und durch die Nacht ihre Augen funkeln. Es wird mich nichts freuen, gar nichts. Alles, was sonst die Leute steigert, extasiert, ruiniert mich totsicher, macht mich still wie die Wand, die Du nicht siehst. Jetzt ziehst Du gar noch zum Herrgott! Gerade so gut kannst Du Dich in Permanenz hängen. Der Herrgott, das ist's. Wir geben ihm all unsere Kraft und können ihn dann nicht mehr ertragen. Ich sehe das immer zu, wie alles ihm zufällt, wie er euch von mir abrückt. Dann bleibe ich übrig, ich gestehe ihm keine Rechte zu, und ich kann nicht sterben, weil ihr an einen Weltfremden glaubt.«

»Du, Giorgio, weisst Du denn, was für eine Frau die Reinheit ist. Du, weisst Du, Frauen ekeln sich meistens vor sich selbst, wenn sie was taugen. Ich will einfach aus all dem Dreck heraus.«

Bebuquin: »In euere grauen, bleiernen Sauermilchtage.«

Euphemia: »In die Erregungen der Seele.«

Bebuquin: »Aber Gott ist ein Wahnsinn.«

Euphemia: »Darum um so fester.

> Genau so wie die menschliche Mathematik, prächtig und leidenschaftlich.
>
> Gott ist die Erregung, die den Körper übertrifft.
>
> Gott ist der Tod, den wir über uns hinaussterben.
>
> Er ist die aufsprossende Vernichtung unserer selbst.
>
> Er ist übermessliche Grösse.
>
> Farbe, die wir noch nicht sahen.
>
> O, wie soll ich ihn tanzen.
>
> Ich müsste Sterne in die Hände raffen.
>
> Sonnen mir unter die Sohlen legen.

Mein Mund sei ein grenzenlos Orchester.

Und das Blech und die Pauke vielfach besetzt.

Ich zerdrücke Trauben in den Fingern.

Und weiss ihn.

Ich liege still und bin weiss wie Mörtel, der die Wände bedeckt,

und kenne Gott.

Er ist der glühend Lauernde in der Dunkelheit.«

Bebuquin: »Er ist der Wahnsinn.

Das Unmögliche.

Der tödlich Auflösende.

Die unfruchtbare Steppe, in die wir kräftige Häuser zwingen.

Die Gefahr für den Willen.

Er ist mein Hass.«

»Bebuquin, halten wir den Atem an. Sie sind ein ganz liebloser Mensch, der nichts opfert, der alles für sich haben will, und das geht nicht. Lassen Sie einiges und nicht zu wenig dem Herrgott. O, ist das nicht Böhm?«

Ihr wurde kalt, dann zog ein feuriger Schweiss über den Körper.

»Hören Sie«, sagte Giorgio, »das ist Unsinn. Schlimm ist es einfach, jedes als Versuchung, als Reiz zu empfinden. Euphemia, heiraten Sie mich doch, es ist sonst nicht zum aushalten.«

»Ja, und jede Nacht schaut Böhm zu, haben Sie denn keine Pietät?«

»Wenn mich was nur so fest hielte, dass ich mich los wäre, irgend ein sympathischer Selbstmord. Meinen Sie, es ist ein Spass, mit mir immer herumzulaufen, und zum reifen Goethe fehlt's mir an Lust und Talent.«

»Glauben Sie, Giorgio, jemand wie Sie bringt kein Weib zwei Zentimeter von der Stelle. Denn sobald Sie etwas tun, ist es gegen Sie. Ich getraue mich nicht gegen Ihren Willen zu sagen, Sie Dressurprodukt.«

Dies redete sie ohne gewärtiges Interesse. So vor vierzehn Tagen hätte sie es noch mit Verve gesagt; denn der Herrgott verlangte sein Recht; und man steigert sich, um zu fallen.

Armer Bebuquin, Du höfliches Tierchen.

Religiöses klingt erotisch vor dem Affenkäfig aus.

Bebuquin irrte mit wundem Hals zwischen den Physiognomien der Häuser. Eine Kokotte tanzte angeheitert an einer Ecke und stapelte ihr vom Frontkorsett aufgetürmtes Posterieur gegen den Sternenhimmel. Euphemia stieg beruhigt und äusserst heilig in eine Nonnenkutte und verliess den Zirkus. Ernst, die Fingernägel polierend, kopfschüttelnd die Straffheit ihrer Brüste hie und da prüfend, begab sie sich gelassen zum Kloster des kostenlosen Blutwunders.

ZWÖLFTES KAPITEL

Bebuquin trat unbemerkt in seine Wohnung. Er kleidete sich sorgfältig um, als er gebadet hatte. Dann ging er isoliert von den Wirrnissen in sein katharktisches Gemach, eine kleine weissgetünchte Stube, inmitten ein Klubsessel.

Er setzte sich bescheiden, dann sagte er:

»O Köstlichkeit der Sünde.

Aber nicht aus infamen Gründen. Es erhebt und stärkt. Sünde verlangt, dass ich alles, was bis zu ihr geschah, vergesse und von vorn anfange. Die Sünde ist ein Tod, und in ihr verbrennt meine Welt. Bisher sind so viele Bebuquins der

Hölle verfallen, und immer reiner und stärker trotz verringerter Kräfte wirft sie mich aus. Vielleicht sündigt man nur, um die Reinheit der Reue zu erlangen, Erneuung durch Gemeinheit.

Jedoch der Schmerz.

Wenn ich an die Sünde denke, kann ich nicht leben. Vergesse ich sie, entschwindet mir nötig mein Leben bis zu diesem Wort, und ich habe es dem Satan zu überantworten.

Gott, wann kann ich mein Lebensende Dir geben?

O beginn mit altem und gezeichnetem Leib zu entraten,

die Identität zu spüren.

Mir starb in dieser Nacht ein Freund.

Meine Gedanken wurden gestrichen.

Die Augen und das Ohr sind sündig.

Was bleibt mir ausser Philosophie;

Denn ich scheine ausserhalb von Prinzipien,

stets böse zu werden.

Braucht meine Gemeinheit so dürre Ruten?«

Er schwieg. In ihm stak eine Höhle, und um ihn herum war der Erdboden ausgesägt. Die Leitung war unterbrochen. Seine Augen lagen reglos über dem Jochbein.

Er sprach:

»O Reichtum meiner Seele,

Vielleicht auch hilflose Vielfältigkeit,

die ich nicht ertragen kann.

Und dann diese Armut.

Es peinigt mich.

Wann verstehe ich, dass man, um zu leben,

um Person zu sein,

nur ein Ding kennen darf. O Reize zu spüren, wie mannigfach Worte und Meinungen sind; und wie schmerzlich, nur eine Deutung zu erlernen. Diese eine Deutung ist die Form, und sie macht die Dinge, die festen Augen, den bestimmten Klang. Wenn ich mich in den Reizen der Mannigfaltigkeit verstecken könnte; und ich weiss nicht, von welchem Zentrum aus ich auferstehen soll.

Herr, der du uns Arbeit gabst, verschone mich mit ihr, damit ich die mögliche Grösse ahne, statt ein geringes Mass zu realisieren. Welch törichte Suggestion, dieses Wort. So liege ich, mit scharfem Ohr wie ein buntes Tier über Deinem Boden, um eine Mitteilung zu erwarten, denn heute habe ich kein Gewand, in dem ich auferstehen könnte.

O Gott, Du gabst uns einen Körper, vielleicht identisch; eine Seele, die den Körper an Möglichkeiten übertrifft, die ihn schon lange Zeit und oft ausrangierte; und die glänzenden Platten der Denker – die Sonne verschmäht es sich in ihnen zu beschauen – suchen die Balance. Ich aber wünsche, dass mein Geist, der sich etwas anderes als diesen Körper – o Gartenzäune, Stadtmauern und Safes, Pensionate und Jungfernhäute – denken will, auch ein Neues wirkt und schafft. Ich kann absonderliche Wesen machen, Verrücktes zeichnen, auf Papier, in Worten, ich selbst bin verzerrt; aber mein Bauch bleibt ein Fresser. Welch geringe Versuche der Heiligen, nach Sprüchen der Evangelien den Körper zu verwandeln.

Herr, gib mir ein Wunder, wir suchen es seit Kapitel eins. Dann will ich normal sein, aber erst dann.

O Gott, wenn Du mehr bist, als das der Wahrheit angenäherte Gesetz der Körper, erbarme Dich doch meiner Langenweile, starb doch schon Böhm an ihr.«

»Bebuquin«, sagte der, »das Ganze ist ein Erziehungsheim. Die drüben sind so menschlich einfach, es gibt zwei Dinge, entweder sie schweigen und machen mit einem imaginären

Phallus unendlich, oder sie tun das Gleiche und zeichnen eine Eins. Ich zeichne eins, und meine isolierte Hirnschale rostet. Ich grüsse Dich, alter Märtyrer. Vernichte die Identität, und Du fliegst rapide; aber fraglich, ob Du das Tempo aushalten wirst. Eins, Hallelujah, eins, Hallelujah, Amen, eins. O Notwendigkeit, Hallelujah, o Gesetz, o Gleichheit, wo alles in sich selbst schläft, o Stille, o Kontemplation, o Verdauung des Straussen, der den eigenen Kot frisst.

Eins, Hallelujah, eins, Hallelujah, leb wohl, eins, Hallel–«

War es Philosophie oder ein Analphabet?

»O Gleichheit, o Eins. Mancher jedoch zählte bis auf zwei. O Erweiterung des Dualismus. O Gehen zwischen den Ufern, o Hinüber- und Herüberrennen.«

Altertum der Gedanken, o Antiquare der Gemeinplätze, o prähistorische Tiefen.

»Seht, mein Leben ist mir verhasst, es ist gänzlich zerstört. Um moralisch weiter zu machen, bedarf ich neuer Existenzbedingungen, eher als des Brotes; ich kann nicht in der Kette weiter leben, ich will nicht, es wäre moralisch inkonsequent. Man treibe mich nicht in die alten Gleise und sei barmherzig, es muss eine Aenderung eintreten, die stärker ist, als meine Sünde und meine Reue; ich muss eine Erneuerung haben, ich bedarf einer Erdperiode.«

Die Nacht färbte langsam empor, die weisse Stube opalisierte wie altes Gestein, lohende Schatten zogen über die Wände, eine kleine weisse Wolke stand vor dem Fenster, ein brennender Sonnenstrahl durchglüht sie. Bebuquins Körper verschwand in den Schatten, nur der Kopf schaute bleich inmitten der Wogen der Dämmerfarben die versinkende Wolke an. Sein Kopf, ein Gestirn, das erkaltete.

DREIZEHNTES KAPITEL

Sterne konkurrieren wiederum vergeblich mit dem bestimmten Licht der Bogenlampen.

»O Kunst«, seufzte Bebuquin, »du bist gewaltig, wenn man Perspektiven wegschickt, ersehnte Veränderung der Zustände, wie ist eine Sache zugleich wahr und falsch, es kommt auf den Standpunkt an.

Versuchung, du tauchst aus der entvölkerten, schlafenden Nacht und erhebst dich aus der Angst vor den Gestirnen.

Ich vergass noch nicht, soweit wie es ziemlich wäre; vielleicht reinigt mich ein anderer, wenn ich's nicht vermag.«

So begab er sich zum Kloster des kostenlosen Blutwunders, nachdenkend, ob eine völlige Unterbrechung des Schicksals möglich sei.

Über ihm, auf den Nadelspitzen der Tannen, glitt Böhm mit.

Der sang:

»Wälder, ihr sympathische Stickerei,

o Schrecken, du Lehrer der Geheimnisse.

Waldfeuer, ihr Offenbarungen im Dickicht.

Irrgänge, Wegschlingen,

gehetzte, angestrengt verirrte Seelen, die ihr sie begeht.«

Seine Hirnkapsel leuchtete den Weg voran mit der nonchalanten Sicherheit eines Toten; er sang weiter:

»Risiko, Wagnisse der Schwachen,

die vergeblich sind,

weil Pappgewichte gestemmt werden,

o philosophische Tricks.

Die gute harmlose Seele eines unwissenden Knaben

geht durch die Wälder.«

Ein Blitz durchfuhr den Wald, der Baum, über den Böhm stieg, schüttelte sich.

Bebuquin hatte grosse Mühe, der Luftreise Böhms nachzukommen, trotzdem dieser recht rücksichtsvoll war; aber oft, wenn Böhm meinte, jetzt müsse es besonders gut gehen, versank Bebuquin im Morast oder stieg keuchend aufwärts, während Böhm die Kugel einer Akazie leicht betanzte.

»O Standpunkte, Vielfältigkeit der Logiker, Kontrapunktik der Sphären«, rief Böhm, sorgfältig das stille Licht seiner Lampe schützend, »die ihr die Dinge zwar vermanscht, doch kaum ruinieren könnt.

Wie entzückt ihr meine Augen,

da ich das fatale Denken mir streng abgewöhnte.

Bebuquin, der Wille zur Dummheit verlangt Entsagung, und man bekommt ihn nur durch sorgfältiges Zuendedenken. Wenn man sieht, dass unsere Gedanken in sich zusammenfallen, wie die Flügel eines geschossenen Wildhuhns; Gedanken, nein, sie sind keine Zwecke für sich, sie sind wert als Bewegung; aber können Gedanken bewegen; o, sie fixieren, sie nageln zu sehr fest, sie konservieren selbst den Revolutionär. Bilder sind Taten der Augen, und mit einem Bilde ist nicht alles gesagt; aber ein Gedanke täuscht stets vor, er habe die ganze Kette erschöpft, und lähmt.

Die Logik will immer eines und bedenkt nicht, dass es viele Logiken gibt. Es gibt nicht Eines, wohl aber eine Tendenz der Vereinheitlichung; und wieviel Dinge streben auseinander. Die Logik hat nicht eine Grundlage. Von ihren vier Axiomen liebt der eine dies, der andere jenes mehr; und ein Axiom befehdet und mischt sich dem anderen; denn eines allein vermag keinen Schritt vorwärts zu gehen; die Logik ist eine ungeheuerliche Ausnahme, und der pythagoreische Lehrsatz ein Monstrum.«

Grüne Drachen mit Schwänzen, die an metallische Sterne dröhnten, fuhren über den Himmel. Staub rieselte gegen den Himmel von der Wüste auf, über die sich Bebuquin schleppte.

Am Horizont stand das Kloster; um es war die unfruchtbare, die stilisierende, dröhnende, vogelüberflogene Wüste gelagert, die Ebene, wo der Blick in rundem Kreis in sich selbst zurückkehrt, um in dem Sand zu versiegen; und die Sonne schlug auf das braune Fell mit den schmetternden Lichtschlägen über die steilen Fanfaren der Felstrümmer hinweg.

VIERZEHNTES KAPITEL

Vor dem Kloster sass ein Mann, in sich selbst schauend. Ueber ihm schwebte eine Frau, man wollte andeuten, was hier geleistet werde, jedoch nur einen geringen Vorgeschmack kosten lassen. Es war das platonische Ehepaar. Er begann sich zu kugeln, indem er den Kopf mit den Füssen umarmte; sie kreiste, sich um sich selbst drehend, über seinem weissen, kurz gescherten Schädel.

Sie litaneierten leise.

»Stille der in sich versunkenen, um sich selbst drehenden Geweihten. Wann steht uns alles in sich selbst? Viele Wege münden in der wundersamen Einsicht, die Idee und die Hurerei; wundgelaufene Füsse und tote Verachtung; knabenhafte unvorsichtige Beschäftigung mit Grenzbegriffen. O infame Unendlichkeit der Faulen, Müden, Tatlosen, Hurer und Bazis, die du sicher ruinierst, die Form zerstörst und die tätige Kraft. O niederträchtiges Versinken in den Punkt der Punkte, in das A O, in den Grund, in den Beschluss.«

Bebuquin ging vorbei und trat in den ekstatischen Vorhof. Es war immer dasselbe. Die Ekstase erregte und steigerte sich an einem Nichts, einer Grube von schwarzem Marmor, worüber man schwebte, in die man schaute, worüber man brütete, in die man schwieg, an der man entbrannte, worin alles verharrte, in die man rief, über der man tanzte, sich geisselte und so fort. Andere hatten statt dessen einen kristallinischen Stein und empfahlen in längeren Reden seine helle Durchsichtigkeit, sein Feuer, seine perspektivische Kraft, seine Brechungen, seine schöpferische Plastik, die Form, die Gefasstheit, die Reinheit und so fort. Um den Stein arbeiteten viele; bald rollte man ihn der schwarzen Grube näher, stülpte ihn darüber, hielt ihn, senkte ihn in die Grube fast bis zum Grund. Die Verzerrungen, die durch den Schliff entstanden, liessen nicht erkennen, ob der Stein in die Grube passe oder nicht. Darum hatte man eine Hypothesen-Kommission, während gemeine Opponenten mit grossen Nasen verlangten, man soll riechen, ob er passte, den Stuhlgang der Riechenden aerostatisch messen und die Kurven, in denen die Exkremente der Riechenden zur Erde fielen, ballistisch berechnen. Ein ziemlich verachteter Teil von Klosternovizen spielte mit einer Maske und einem Spiegel, aber davon soll man nicht reden. Aus einem kleinen Säulengang klang die leiernde Stimme eines Bonzen.

»Ich und Du sind eines, diese Identität hält die Welt zusammen. Die Kontemplation ist eine phantastische Fähigkeit; denn sie geht über die Dinge hinweg in eine geistige Gemeinschaft. Es ist ein Grundgefühl über den Satz des Widerspruchs. In meiner glühenden Liebe ist B gleich A. Grund und Folge fallen in eins. Jedes kehrt ins andere zurück, um sich selbst zu finden. O gleiche Kraft, o Geschehnislosigkeit, o Ereignisse, höchst eindeutig.«

Bebuquin schrie: »Hier wird ein sanktionierter Selbstmord vollzogen, hier wird sakrale Idiotie gezüchtigt, Augen ausgerissen. Mein Herr, ich kam gerade hierher, um einen neuen Menschen zu fabrizieren. Ich lebe nur noch vom Wort anders. Ich kann die Gleichheit nicht gebrauchen.«

Der Bonze rief ihm zu:

»Werden Sie der Erscheinung nach anders. Übrigens ist es ganz belanglos, was Sie meinen. Sie sind ja nur Urgrund, darum innerst sündlos.«

Bebuquin schimpfte.

»Mich interessiert der Urgrund gar nicht, ich pfeife darauf.«

Böhm trat ihm entgegen in gelber Mönchskutte.

»Eine Hoffnung besteht, Bebuquin; die Verwandlung tritt vielleicht mit dem Tode ein. Entweder wir bleiben dort, was wir sind, oder wir werden vernichtet und verwandelt.«

Bebuquin: »Aber ist es nicht möglich, sich im Leben zu wandeln, das elende Gedächtnis zu verlieren?«

»Bebuquin, du bist an dir erkrankt. Die Sünde ruht nicht nur im Gedächtnis, sondern auch in der Tat, die unter den Menschen und im Himmel umhergeht.«

»Aber muss man denn sterben, um anders zu werden?«

»Beichten Sie und opfern Sie sich. Ich glaubte, das Phantastische genüge, ich wurde lackiert, gehen Sie, beichten Sie.«

Bebuquin rief beichtend in das Tor der Kapelle:

»Ich verzichte darauf, durch eine Reinigung reduziert und entleert zu werden. Ich verpöne es, in Armut von vorn anzufangen. Ich will irgend ein anderes Schicksal, ich sah mein Schicksal, es ist nichts als die Wiederholung einer Dummheit. Ich bitte, dass es mir gelinge, von den vielen Dingen, die ich mir vorzustellen vermag, eins zu sein.«

Der Beichtiger rief erwidernd aus dem Inneren der Kapelle:

»Sie stellen sich vieles vor. Sinnvoll aber sind nur Vorstellungen, mit denen man handeln kann. Sie bedürfen der Grundverwandlung, die aber ist der Tod.«

Bebuquin: »Viele Dinge geschehen, die nicht einzuordnen sind, verworfen oder nicht gesehen werden, verdeckt von der tödlichen Vernunft.«

Strophe: »Petrefakte Bäume meines Gartens spiegeln sich im blinden Kristallboden;

die Bewegung meiner Hände fährt nur in die Ruhe;

jedes Brennen, Fliegen, Reissen

wird versteint.

Zum schlafenden Gebirge fügen sich die Tage an;

und je toter, desto fester,

unvergänglicher, steiler,

unübersteiglicher hemmt mich das Bleibende,

die Vergangenheit.«

Antiphone: »Der Fähige bildet Vergangenes um, im Wechsel seiner Gegenwart und Zukunft; und diese wandelt sich, gewinnt auch an Beziehungen, und fruchtlos, ja schädlich wird es im zehnten Jahr das Glück und einzige Lösung.«

Strophe: »Was in Erinnerung steht, ist verlorene Kraft und Hemmung, Bindung zu gleichen Sünden. Was gewesen ist, wirkt wie die Schablone, wir stehen in dem Fluss, immer brodelt das gleiche Wasser.«

Man sprach in einer leichten Unterhaltung weiter. Bebuquin meinte:

»Sehen Sie, die Logik fixiert, soweit unsere Fähigkeiten auf sogenannte Tatsachen angewendet werden. Sie bedenkt nur unsere praktischen Bedürfnisse, richtet sich nach den Dingen und sucht diese in übereinstimmenden, sich wiederholenden Beziehungen zu erhalten. Aber in mir ist so viel und gerade das Wertvollste, was über die Tatsache hinausgeht. Die materielle Welt und unsere Vorstellungen decken sich nie. Darum ist die Tat notwendig, dies Correktiv von Tatsachen und Dingen. Wenn man jedoch wie ich zu der Überzeugung gelangte, dass wir weiter müssen, dass wir uns verwandeln müssen; ist es dann nicht möglich, dass eine neue Art Mensch entsteht, die es verschmäht, in den gleichen Strassen weiter zu gehen?«

Trompeten und Pauken schollen von der Decke der Kapelle. Bebuquin trat in sie ein. Er sprach weiter:

»Bisher wurde das Religiöse an den Tatsachen zur Groteske, oder umgekehrt; aber vielleicht decken sich die Dinge nie, damit das Schöpferische nicht einschlafe. Gott, das Phantastische, die ganze unterdrückte, sprachlose Sensibilität wollen reden, wir sträuben uns gegen diese immer gleiche Auslese, die Welt muss sich uns verwandeln.«

FÜNFZEHNTES KAPITEL

Bebuquin soll in der folgenden Nacht lange und im Zusammenhange gesprochen haben. Er sagte in der Leere des Zimmers:

»Ich beginne die Rede vom Tod im Leben, von der grossen Ruhe, von der reinen Armut und der leeren Lauterheit.

Eins geht durchs Leben und ist sehr lebendig, das bist Du, allzuhäufiges Wort Nein. Aber eins steht und wird sehr geachtet, o Ruhe.

Ich weiss, du bist verführerisch wie die Tiefe des Wassers für junge Mädchen, die am Morgen unter Vermischtem gedruckt sind.

Du bist sicher die Mutter der Vollendung und der Vater der Metaphysik; denn nur in der Ruhe ist Festigkeit und dauerndes Ende,

Ist stete Isolierung, und es wird nichts vermischt.

Ich aber stehe und fluche dir,

du Müdigkeit, die mir Gedanken und Augen betäubtest,

meine schnellen Füsse versanden liessest;

du müdes Hirn und träges Blut,

die ihr nicht mal den Tod erwartet,

ihr Gleichgültigen.

Der aber ist ins Leben verwickelt,

und jeder Tag Mühe und Wachstum ist ein Tag Tod.

Und wer mag von beiden Recht behalten? Ich glaube, sie beide sind sich gleich und eines, und das Leben hebt sich selbst auf.

Du totes Leben!

Der Platoniker, der denkt, diskutiert, und sein mühsam Ziel eine Sicherheit und Ruhe.

Ziele erregen die Kraft und beenden sie.

Wer weiss, ob die gefundene Idee mehr fördert als bewegt.

Sie stärkt vielleicht dich, primitive Sicherheit, dich, Geist, ich verbeuge mich nicht;

doch er lehrt den Toren, um Dich hundert Dinge verachten.

Und ich sah nur, dass ein Mensch ein Kräftewirbel ist, von dem einiges ausfliesst, und anderes geht in ihn ein, bis Du, Ruhe, kommst.

O Reinheit, was sagst Du anderes, als, Du erträgst nur Geringes.

Und die Lehre von der Armut meint dasselbe.

Ihr seid sehr hohe Erkenntnisse gewesen.

Tod und Endlichkeit, du bist der Erzeuger unserer Arbeit, du treibst uns zur Mühe, und vielleicht bist du der Vater des Lebens, und dies keimt gering nur vor Dir auf.

Du lässt die Gestirne leuchten und zeigst unsere geringe Kraft; denn Mond und Sonne scheinen einander zu in notwendiger Umarmung. Wir jedoch können nur nach einem Gestirn handeln, und dem Auge sind sie sich ausschliessende Gegensätze.

Tod, du bist der Vater der Zeugung, und du gabst uns Menschen alles Endliche, bestätigst unsere Sinne, welche Formen sehen, hören, schmecken und bejahst die Ahnung des vielleicht dilettantischen Geistes, damit wir sehen dürfen und eines schauen – damit wir denkend nichts sehen.

Ich bin ein Vollstrecker für Dich, Tod. Ich will es sagen, dass nur Gestorbene sterben; wenn einer jung und kräftig stirbt, vielleicht stirbt er für einen anderen.

Du gabst uns Begierden und Ziele, und wir wehren uns gegen Dich durch Zeitloses, durch seiende Ideen, durch den Anspruch auf Totalität. Aber vielleicht sind das deine geringsten Formen.

Tod, du Vater des Humors, wenn dich ein Wunder, das ich mit meinen Augen sehe, vernichtete;

dein Feind ist das Phantastische, das ausser den Regeln steht;

aber die Kunst zwingt es zum stehen, und erschöpft gewinnt es Form.

Ich nenne dich, Tod, den Vater der Intensität, den Herrn der Form.

So steht es für dieses Leben.«

Die Nacht trat in die Stube.

Ein alter Mann kam in die Stube; er sprach:

»Verzeihen Sie, ich wohne seit langem unter Ihnen, es fällt mir sehr schwer zu sprechen, bin es seit langem nicht mehr gewohnt.

Ich komme nur, um zu sagen: ich bin seit langem tot durch meinen Willen; ich lebte nur scheinbar, seien Sie bitte dabei, um zu konstatieren, dass ich den Tod hintergangen habe. Ich sterbe als der grösste Humorist.«

Der alte Herr sank zusammen, er war ruhig und starr. Dann schrie er laut auf und sagte:

»Der war doch schlimmer, ich betrog nur das Leben und mich.«

Bebuquin trug den Leichnam in die Wohnung des Alten. Er schaute ihn ein längeres an, dann ging er in seine Wohnung.

Er schaute durch das Fenster zur breiten Baumallee hinunter, einige Menschen kamen mühselig wandernd vorüber und riefen:

»Das Gesetz ist die grosse tötende Ausnahme, wir gehen in den Dingen, die Wunder zu suchen.«

Bebuquin wandte sich vom Fenster ab, der Mond schien ihm sein erstauntes Loch in den Rücken, er setzte sich hin, schaute auf seine Hände, die noch nie gearbeitet hatten, und sprach lange.

»Gleichgültigkeit, woraus bist Du wohl gewebt, war die allzu grosse Empfindlichkeit Dein Ursprung, oder die Kraft, die der opulenten Natur gleichkommt? Ich sah schon viele aus Gleichgültigkeit die absonderlichsten Capricen begehen, und schon mancher war es aus Furcht vor der eigenen Wut. O Erstarrnis, stagnierender Tod; Versteinerung und Schlaf, ihr fristet uns das Leben, das sich wütend aufbrauchte ohne eure Hemmung.

O Krankheit, komme, nur du kannst mir Grenzen geben, Gott lass mich einen ungeheuren Schmerz empfinden, damit der Geist paralysiert werde; oder vielleicht, o Hoffnung, schafft die Krankheit einen neuen Körper, fähig zu den sonderlichen Dingen, deren ich bedarf.

Herr, ich weiss, am Ende eines Dinges steht nicht sein Superlativ, sondern sein Gegensatz, und die Erkenntnisse gehen zum Wahnsinn. Ich bin geschaffen zu erkennen und zu schauen, aber Deine Welt ist hierzu nicht gemacht; sie entzieht sich uns; wir sind weltverlassen. Suchen wir Dich, o Gott, dann sterben wir in der lautlosen Erstarrung, und es ist keine Erkenntnis, sondern Du bist das Ende.

Herr, lass mich einmal sagen,

ich schuf aus mir.

Sieh mich an, ich bin ein Ende, lass mich eine unabhängige Tat, ein Wunder tun.

O Nacht der Verwandlung, wann kommst du, wo ich diesen Körper vergesse, ja, ihn abstreife, und die Dinge anderes bedeuten und anderes sind, denn je sonst; die Glieder werden selbstständig, die Teile beginnen zu reden. Die Auflösung, sie ist die Verwandlung und sei mir ein Anfang.«

SECHZEHNTES KAPITEL

Bebuquin trat steif in die neblige Nacht. Die Reflexe der Bogenlampen stürmten durch die Baumäste und schwammen wie breite opalisierende Fische in dem nassen Boden. Bebuquin stand ein Ausrufezeichen. Er lief, rannte durch eine Prozession irgendwelcher neuen Sektierer; verschiedene Messiasse, dekorative junge Mädchen rannte er um; es galt, in den Zirkus zu gelangen. Er musste aus sich Aeusserungen solcher künstlichen unlogischen Bewegungen abzwingen, um zunächst die Physik mit der Kraft seines absterbenden Akts zu widerlegen.

Er ging in eine Loge des Zirkus.

Etwas Sonderliches geschah.

Während eines Radlertriks fuhr eine spiegelnde Säule in die Arena, blitzend; eine Flötenbläserin ging nebenher in einer Nonnenkutte. Die Bürger sahen sich darin, bald strahlend übergross, bald verzerrt; diese Spiegel zwangen, immer wieder hineinzuschauen. Mäuler schluckten die Arena, und die Finsternis aufgerissener Gurgeln verdunkelte sie. Die Blicke versuchten; die hohe Spiegelsäule zu durchbrechen. Ein Weib stürzte aufgewölbten Rocks hinunter unter dem Druck des neugierigen Staunens. Eine Gallerie brach durch; inmitten die Spitzen der unermüdlichen Finger der Bläserin und die Spiegel, die mit dem Schatten der andern sprechend tanzten. Die Säule trat in die Schatten geschwungenen Sprunges.

Die Menschen verwandelten sich in sonderliche Zeichen in den Spiegeln; das Publikum wurde leise irrsinnig und richtete in drehendem Schwindel seine Bewegungen nach denen der Spiegel; um die Spiegel sausten farbige Reflektoren.

Eine innerste Dunkelheit, ein Lichtblitz, der in die Mauer zurückfuhr, eine Anzahl sprang von den Gallerien.

Ein junger Mann fuhr zur Decke ins Freie hinaus.

»Bagage« rufend.

Das Publikum raste weiter, die Verzerrung für wahr haltend.

Bis in die öde Frühe.

Die Paralyse zog in die Stadt ein.

Mehrere Eisenbahnwaggons hielten mittags vor dem Zirkus.

Im friedlichen Sonnenschein sortierte man die Toten aus.

Dann verlud man die Irren.

In der Stadt war ein halb Jahr Fasching. Bürger leisteten Bedeutendes an Absurdität. Ein grotesker Krampf überkam die meisten. Ein bescheidener Spass war's, sich gegenseitig die Hirnschale einzuschlagen. Die Raserei wurde dermassen schmerzlich, dass man begann zu töten.

Man begann mit einem Alten, der als Pierrot angezogen an einem Wegweiser bei den Füssen aufgehängt wurde.

Ein Mädchen, das noch einen Rest Vernunft besass, schrie, »hier stirbt der Allmensch« und bat, sie gleichfalls zu hängen; denn sie sei Mörder und Gehängter schon ohnehin, dank ihrer ethischen Sensibilität.

Sie wurde unter nicht unbedeutenden Greueln beinlings gehängt. Jedoch verübelte man ihr, dass sie keine gute Unterwäsche trug. Verschiedene Messiasse traten mit Erfolg auf, Messiasse der Reinheit, der Wollust, des Pflanzenessens, des Tanzes, hypnotisierende Messiasse und einige andere. Hatte man genug Anhänger, so wurde die Sache langweilig. Überlebte Messiasse verwandte man als Redakteure, zumal ihnen Sensation geläufig war. Die neue Weltanschauung kristalisierte sich zur Ziege, die ein Bein gebrochen hat.

Vor dem Fenster Bebuquins tauchten einige Irre auf. Er neigte sich heraus, die Glatze von der Mittagssonne beleuchtet. Die Fratzen sprangen am Fenster hoch wie Gummibälle, einer schrie »Gib uns wieder zurück, lass uns heraus, nimm die Spiegel weg«, denn der gleissende Schrecken der Spiegel hing über der Stadt.

SIEBZEHNTES KAPITEL

Euphemia besuchte Bebuquin. Sie klopfte an der Tür. Beinern knackte der Gruss.

Er rief von Innen, »er ist nicht da, kam sich abhanden.«

Sie trat ein.

»Euphemia, die einen ziehen sich zusammen, verkrumpeln; ich platze ein rasend Sich-Verlieren.

Wie war ich dicht und scharf, schneidend wie ein Florett mit vielen Kurven. Man wird einfach und stumpf.

O zuckender Blitz, o stehende gerinnende Funsel.

Ich hätte auf mir stehen müssen, auf der eigenen Stecknadel, mich stumm in mich bohrend, bis die strahlende Spitze aus dem Hirn heraus spriesst, blitzend, und der Schädel futsch ist.

Man muss den Mut zu seinem privaten Irrsinn haben, seinen Tod zu besitzen und zu vollstrecken.

Menschen, die zum Irrsinn geschaffen sind, die sich mit normalen Weibern bekämpfen, den gebährenden Gemeinplätzen.«

Euphemia sagte, auf dicken Beinen stehend, lieblich breit grinsend, mütterlich banalisierend, abtötend:

»Du kennst keine Güte.«

Er: »Die ruiniert mich, wer lässt mich, wie ich sein muss?«

Sie: »Du hast so zu sein, dass Du die Verantwortung für Kinder übernehmen kannst.«

»Aber mit mir wird Schluss gemacht.«

Blödsinnig lange, dumme, gähnende Schatten schlossen ihn ein.

»Der Tod«, schrie sie.

»Verzeihung, zweimal zwei ist vielleicht immer vier, dann geht es weiter; vielleicht auch nicht, dann ist es Schluss.«

Sie: »Die Zahl ist keine Tatsache, sie ist nur eine Ordnung und steht ausser der Seele.«

Die Lichter eines Autos sausten durch die Stube.

»Reisst mich weg«, schrie er; Wände waren da, und Glasfenster schneiden.

»Man wehrt sich gegen sich selbst, hat nicht den Mut zu sich. Wer von den beiden ist Er? Einer davon ist mir verhasst, widerlich; der andere furchtbar, kopfüber in die Wirrnis.«

Böhm breitete sich an der Decke aus. Ein breiter Schatten mit Lichtklexen, seine Augen stechende Kerzen, er schwoll beim Sprechen an, ein schall-geblähtes Segel.

»Kopuliert euch, diskutiert nichts Besseres vor dem Selbstverständlichen oder nehmt Rasiermesser.«

»Böhm, ich steile in Dich. Böhm, was ist das alles?«

Der rollte sich durch den oberen Ritz des Fensters hinaus, stieg sorgfältig in den Reflexstrahl einer Laterne, rief im Lichtkern »Oho!«

Bebuquin sagte:

»Ich hätte mich und die Welt ohne Laster nicht ertragen, nicht ohne den Willen gegen mich, nicht ohne partiellen Selbstmord. Der ist nötig wie das sogenannte Positive. Alles wäre mir sonst Geist, Willkür und grenzenlos, und das läuft zum Ende auf die grosse Oper hinaus.«

Euphemia: »Bebuquin, bei Dir bin ich noch nie auf die Kosten gekommen. Lagen wir zusammen, kommt Dir die Philosophie, und das ist sehr komisch. Man kann sich bei Dir gar nicht ernst nehmen, ein Kontrast frisst den andern auf.«

Heinrich Lippenknabe trat ein.

»Ah, Kontrast, so heftig wie möglich. Aber man ordne ihn dem Gesetz unter. Das Gesetz ist Freiheit, und sie verwandelt den Kontrast zur Harmonie.«

Eine dicke Dame schwebt ein, geht mit dem Busen.

»Und man muss die Harmonie geniessen, alles zur Freude auflösen, zu einer behaglichen Seligkeit. Wenn man so vollendet ist wie ich …«

Bebuquin wirft die Dame zum Fenster hinaus. Lippenknabe springt ihr nach, kommt früher zu Boden, beide fallen in ein Waschbottich; er verkauft ihr vor dem Heraussteigen ein Bild, sie feilschen vor Wasser triefend, fontänen-gleich unter dem antiken Himmel.

Bebuquin sprach leise zu Euphemia.

»Alles kommt auf den Tod an. Ist's hier zu Ende, dann können wir nicht vollendet werden. Kommt es denn auf mehr als den einzelnen Menschen an; und geht es weiter, dann ist auch dies Leben nur hinderlich. Auf dieser Erde einen Zweck haben, ist lächerlich.

Zwecke sind immer jenseits, darüber hinaus; also wir brauchen ein Jenseits, glauben es aber nicht, und schliesslich, ein Jenseits ist kraftraubend. Zwei Methoden gibt's, entweder man glaubt und ist bei Gott, ist Mystiker und verblödet an einer nagelnden Idee fixe, oder man platzt und wird gesprengt. Immer ist der Wahnsinn das einzig vermutbare Resultat.«

Euphemia: »Warum?«

»Diese Wünsche, die in mir sausen wie Tramways, die mich mir entreissen, ich bin vom Getöse der Nichtigkeiten umlärmt.«

Unten schlürften betropfte Enthusiasten weiter; der Maler predigte der dicken Dame von abstinenz, der heroischen Einsamkeit und der Tragik des Schaffenden; damit sie ihn harmonisiere.

O, ihr gefetteten Stimmen der Nacht, wandelnd durch nebelathmende Alleen, Ursache lyrischer Bände, Gelegenheit dekorativen Schreitens mit dem Blick in jene Fernen gesenkt, torkelnd über Plätze; man scherze über das verklungene Spiel der Kinder.

ACHTZEHNTES KAPITEL

»Wir haben Böhm zu begraben«, rief Bebuquin, »der Kerl wird lästig.«

Um die Leiche des Teuren, eine öffentliche Angelegenheit, kümmerte man sich nicht; wollte ihn nur erledigen.

Bebuquin stieg aus der Bar, von der Möglichkeit eines Begräbnisses überzeugt.

Die Leiche irgendeines Selbstmörders wurde vorbeigetrottet, dahinter ein trauernder, leerer Repräsentationswagen.

Bebuquin stieg ein und murmelte. Man kam zum Stadtende, wo die letzten Häuser erfolglos die Ebene zu akzentuieren suchten, hielt am Kirchhof.

Bebuquin schlich sich ungesehen herein.

Er fand eine unbenutzte Stelle, zögerte jedoch noch, das Grab aufzuwerfen; dann ging er daran mit heftiger Wut. Wie er einigermassen ein Loch zustande gebracht hatte, war die übrige Amtshandlung zu Ende. Er grub weiter, stellte sich als Monument hinter die Grube, des öfteren den Grabspruch sagend:

»Weinet inniglich und seid gebückt!«

Und faltete die Hände über die Brust.

Die Sonne ging auf und funkelte auf ihn, der als Gekreuzigter dastand.

Allmählich ging diese Stellung in ein geregeltes Freiturnen über.

»Stofflosigkeit, Stofflosigkeit«, knirschte er vor Wut und begab sich zum Grab einer gewissen Josefine Peters, geborene Dewitz, um heisse Tränen zu vergiessen.

NEUNZEHNTES KAPITEL

Bericht der letzten drei Nächte.

Erste Nacht. – Bebuquin lag ruhig in den weissen Kissen, lang ausgestreckt, lange ein Loch in die Decke stierend, welche sich nicht hob. Kurze Zeit meinte er im Schlamm zu schwimmen; dann fieberte er, sich den Kopf mit den Fingern umfassend; ziemlich ängstlich versteckte er sich vor dem offenen Fenster. Er war nicht fähig zu sprechen. Nach einer Stunde redete er sehr beherrscht.

Zweite Nacht. – Bebuquin vermied es einzuschlafen, wohl die Träume fürchtend. Es sei Gefahr, meinte er, dass er zu sehr ins Träumen gerate. Er spricht sehr erregt und spürt um sich dunkle Vögel flattern. Dann erstarren die Kiefer.

Dritte Nacht. – Bebuquin schlief ruhig ein, fuhr im Schlaf einigemal mit den Händen empor; sein Gesicht lag allmählich wie im Krampf, die Haut faltete sich und umrunzelte den ganzen Schädel. Ruckweise öffneten sich auf Sekunden seine Lider, er zog Finger und Zehen sich spreizend in die Länge, dann ging er eng zusammen und zitterte heftig. Gegen Morgen wachte er auf, war unfähig zu reden und konnte nicht mehr allein essen. Nur einmal schaute er kühl drein und sagte

Aus.

ALSO IN THIS SERIES

Carl Einstein, *Negro Sculpture*,
translated by Patrick Healy (print, 2016 – ebook, 2014).

Karl Kraus, *The Last Days of Mankind: A Tragedy in Five Acts*,
translated by Patrick Healy (print and ebook 2016).

Karl Kraus, *In These Great Times: Selected Writings*,
translated by Patrick Healy (print, 2017 – ebook, 2014).

Else Lasker-Schüler, *My Heart: A Novel of Love*,
translated by Sheldon Gilman and Robert Levine
(print and ebook, 2016).

Max Raphael, *The Invention of Expressionism: Critical
Writings 1910-1913*, translated by Patrick Healy (print 2017).

Walter Rheiner, *Cocaine: Selected Writings*,
translated by Bradley Schmidt and Gijs van Koningsveld
(print, 2017– ebook, 2014).

IN PREPARATION

Albert Ehrenstein, *Tubutsch*,
translated by Gijs van Koningsveld.